For my brother Chad
Who has always encouraged me to explore

Syndrome

Published by Nicho Young

Published 2024

First edition published 2021, Second edition published 2024.

ISBN: 979-8-9878657-3-6

SYNDROME

SEPTEMBER 13

SYNDROME

1

The ringing in Detective Vincent Aronson's head would not stop. Even after waking from the dreadful dream, he couldn't stop the vibration passing through his ear canals and rattling his brain. He opened and closed his mouth silently in an attempt to equalize the pressure, but the noise persisted. His consciousness slowly came into focus as he remembered his liquid meal the night before; an appetizer of bourbon, followed by the main course, a six pack of beer, and then drinking half a bottle of wine for dessert. As he replayed it in his head, he felt dinner trying to resurface, but he cleared his throat and breathed slowly until the nausea passed.

Finally, the ringing stopped, and Vincent sat up, watching his room spin the opposite direction as he did. He figured he was still a bit drunk and ran his hand over his face a few times, a half-hearted attempt to sober up. His eyes did not want to stay open, but he knew he needed to start his day or he would lie in bed until the next.

The buzzing began again, but this time Vincent looked over at his bedside table and saw his cell phone skittering across it, nearing the edge. The caller I.D. told him it was Detective Lewis Monroe. He sighed, and almost retched again after inhaling his own toxic fumes. Reaching for the phone, the world tilted once more, but he grabbed it as he fell onto the floor of the only bedroom in his cabin, secluded in the woods. He waited for his head to steady and the new clatter in his ears to dwindle. Only then did he answer the phone.

"It's my day off, Lew. I'm not available."

"Vince, I don't give a shit if you're on another planet, which it sounds like you actually might be. I need you to get to the edge of the forest in Angel's Rest. Now!"

The tone of Lew's voice was one of excitement and nervous energy, and Vince made a hearty attempt at sobering up quickly.

"Lew, I'm gonna be honest with you. I kind of tied one on last night and I don't think it's safe for me to drive."

Vince *knew* it wasn't safe for him to drive, but he was trying to be congenial about the interruption to his morning. He looked at the clock and corrected himself, his afternoon.

"Take a goddamn Uber if you have to, I just need you down here ASAP."

Vince could hear the exasperation in Lew's voice, but he still felt he would be worthless at a crime scene.

"There's a lot of edge of the forest in the Rest, Lew. Where exactly am I supposed to be going?"

There was no response. Vince sighed again, resignation in his voice.

"Seriously? I'm taking my day off."

He was about to end the call when Lew responded.

"I called you an Uber, now get your ass over here and assist us with this. No more arguments. Grab some breath mints if you need to." He was gone before Vince could respond.

Vince stood up, feeling his stomach lurch dangerously, and just as he thought he was going to get away with keeping the contents of his stomach where they belonged, his body betrayed him, and he started to dry heave. He barely opened the lid of the toilet before spewing its contents into the bowl; last night's meal and what appeared to be an after-dinner snack he had no recollection of eating.

2

The Uber driver pulled up in front of Vince's house mere moments after he tucked away his hip flask and concealed with his jacket his shoulder holster holding his personal Glock. Normally, he would keep his service pistol on his waistband along with his badge, but it was his day off and he had no intention letting this take up his whole day.

His cabin sat at the end of a cul-de-sac, down a short drive under a grove of oak trees. It was the perfect place to raise a family. That had, in fact, been the plan all along, but the divorce came before the babies, so spit on that for now. The place served its purpose well enough for Vince, and he figured maybe someday he could hang up his vices and start afresh with all new ones. It backed up to about a thousand acres of woodlands. His property extended nearly ten acres into that wood, and he had hidden a pole barn and woodshed just out of eyesight. Being a detective in a tri-city region where half the people you interrogate are people you went to high school with or their parents or kids, one needed a little getaway in case things got hairy.

The man in the Uber, more a kid really, looked down at his phone and looking up, tapped the switch to roll down his window.

"You Lew?"

Vince shook his head and walked toward the car, a little electric-gas hybrid job that probably got a hundred miles to the gallon.

"I'm Detective Aronson. Lew is my partner. He called you for me."

He could see the hesitation in the young man's eyes, so he pulled the edge of his jacket back to reveal his badge. "Police business."

"That's a nice belt, but your name isn't on the pickup list." The young man lifted his cell phone to his face and began chewing on the inside of his cheek.

It took Vince a moment to remember he had left his badge in the house, but by the time he turned to go retrieve it the young man was speaking with someone.

"Hi. Yes. Is this Lew? Yeah, I am here, but the guy isn't on the pickup list. That's okay. It happens." The young man tried to lower his voice to talk business with Lew, but Vince still heard every word of what came next.

"Listen, you know there is a cleanup fee, right? I mean, your pal here is looking like he's about to blow chunks all over." The driver's eyes wandered briefly in Vince's direction, making Vince shift uncomfortably while he wrapped up the phone call and waved the Detective over.

"Everything good?" Vince asked, trying not to sound irritated, but failing miserably.

"Yeah, man. Errr, Detective."

The young man now looked nervous, and he jumped a little when Vince walked to the front passenger door and climbed inside. He smiled over at Vince and then they were off to the races.

3

The ride was silent, and Vince took the opportunity to try and gain his bearings so he could be of some help when he got to the scene. Something had agitated Lew and it wasn't like him to call Vince in on a day off. In fact, Lew had refused to call Vince on the rare occasion he was late for work. There was an unspoken understanding between the partners. They both knew the other had downfalls, but the work they did together more than compensated for their indiscretions. The two had worked together for nearly two decades and, of course, others around the station referred to them as the old married couple, which didn't bother either of them. In fact, it seemed to give them a certain level of immunity where they could get away with more than others at the precinct. If something sloppy happened with one of them, their coworkers assumed the other one would handle it and put it to rest. And that was what normally happened. Every once in a while, there would be a little spill over, but for the most part they were treated like separate entities.

Detective Lewis Monroe was a never married, never wanted to marry man who enjoyed the company of as many ladies as he deemed necessary to have a good time. He once bragged to Vince that he was with three women at once, and Lew made the mistake of naming the three women, two of whom Vince knew personally. Vince, naturally, checked with those two women to see if the stories were true. Lew hadn't spoken to Vince for nearly a month after that incident, but it sobered him up to stop telling tales out of school regarding his sex life, or lack thereof.

For all of Vince's shortcomings, he had a way of letting others see themselves in a new light. It was what made him a good detective.

The number of confessions he had gotten from 'persons of interest' who were too stubborn to speak with anyone else, numbered in the hundreds. Facial tics, nervous eye movements, jittery legs, anything he could use against the person he was interrogating to get the information he wanted. He was known around the precinct as the Cold Case King, which had less to do with actual cold cases and more strictly meant he could solve nearly any case that had turned frigid in one sense or another.

Lew had joined the force when he was nineteen, taking after his father before him who was the sheriff of the tri-cities before they had split *into* the tri-cities. It took him a year to make detective, and Vince took him under his wing, having a whole year head start on the Detective front. Lew was the youngest Detective the state had ever hired, and that would likely remain the case for the rest of eternity, mainly due to the strings that were pulled to get him the position. Sometimes small jurisdictions in the middle of nowhere tended to play by their own rules. Vince didn't mind. The kid was sharp and willing to put in the hours to excel at the job. Sure, he was immature, but who wasn't as they rounded the bases into their twenties. And the partnership was a good one and had earned not only them, but the entire precinct multiple commendations on jobs well done. Their successful arrest rate and subsequent correct conviction rate was well above the average for anywhere else in the country.

So, if Lew had broken his normal protocol and called Vince on his day off, he knew there was something more than a dead dog in someone's backyard. It wasn't like they got many cases that would even make the local papers, but they had solved a serial killer case a few years back and had broken up a start-up DIY drug ring that was selling kids a tainted ecstasy strain they were calling EZ Does It. Twelve kids had died before they shut down the entire operation, which was a guy and a couple buddies who were working out of a small barn on someone else's property. And, in reality, it had been the duffer whose property was being used that broke the case wide open. Vince had been at the local bar, winding his way into oblivion, when he heard the old guy talking about how there were some real funny smells wafting through his property lately, and he was fairly certain it wasn't a paper mill. That lucky break ended the venture post haste, but Vince and Lew never told anyone else it was sheer, dumb luck that cinched that one up tight. They were sure they would have eventually figured it out, but meanwhile more kids would have probably died.

The Uber pulled up to the scene, which already had yellow tape flapping in the wind, and it looked like nearly the entire precinct was on site. The young man driving the car let out a low whistle.

He turned to Vince with a look of pure curiosity and said, "Good luck out there. If you need any help, I watch a lot of police shows. I know a few things."

Vince opened the car door and exited, grabbing for his wallet. He held out a few dollars to the driver. "Most of those shows are inaccurate. But I'll keep you in mind."

The young man grabbed the tip and thanked Vince as the Detective walked toward the scene. He did turn enough to stare at the young man lingering, probably hoping to get a glance at something he could relay to his pals later that night. The driver sped off, tires screeching slightly, the red embarrassment slowly creeping up his face.

4

Vince had taken no more than three steps when he saw Lew rushing toward him with a look that relayed horrified excitement. Lew grabbed his arm and started word-vomiting all the information he could get out before they got to the actual scene.

"Early this morning a man was jogging along the ravine, and he heard a sound. He described it like a sort of squalling animal. Who uses the word squalling? Some sort of woodland creature in extreme pain. So, like any dimwitted moron, his curiosity overcame him, and he decided to investigate. Coulda been a cougar mauling a fox, or a kid torturing a rabbit. Coulda been anything."

They weaved their way through the forensics team and a few deputies that looked like they had seen a body going through a mulcher.

Lew continued to spew his story, "And this guy. This..." he struggled to find a word to describe the gentleman who came across whatever it was they were approaching, "This treasure of a human being walked up to the edge of the woods and lost his lunch. Breakfast. Whatever. Anyhow, he chucked all over the ground and then decided to call us to come check out what he found."

Lew always was a fan of the dramatic, so he waited until Vince asked the inevitable question before continuing. "And what did he find, Lew?"

A twisted grin flashed across Lew's face, and he winked at Vince, "You'll see."

Vince sighed, his stomach rumbling impatiently. "Why you gotta do it like that? Just tell me. You know I hate suspense."

But Lew was undeterred in this irritating little game and simply smiled that wicked smile again. They stepped over the crest of the slight hill that lay before the edge of the forest and as the ground came into view Vince saw something he couldn't have ever anticipated, not in all of his wild musings, even given a hundred years with a thousand clues. The carnage that lay before him instantly turned his stomach and he dry heaved three times before standing back up, wiping tears from his eyes.

"What the hell happened here?"

Across the grassy knoll that bordered the forest there were streaks of blood. Partially congealed gobs dripped off the ends of long strands of grass, stringing out like deep red saliva. There were spots where pools of blood had formed, and within those pools were dead animals. Correction, dead animal parts. A leg here, a head there, at least fifteen animals could be accounted for based on the ripped apart torsos. And when Vince took a closer look, it seemed that each of the torsos had been eviscerated; torn from stem to stern; all the organs removed. Looking around, he couldn't find a single organ anywhere. They were gone. It was as if someone came in, butchered the animals and then set off somewhere else to perhaps make a nice pot of innards stew.

Lew patted him on the back. "Yeah, I probably shoulda warned ya about all this. But at least you got it all out of your system. Let's get a closer look, shall we?"

Lew took off, not waiting around to see if Vince was following.

Of course, Vince followed. Slowly at first and then, despite his trepidations, he caught up to Lew and his detective brain kicked into gear.

"So, why is this a big deal if someone came out here and butchered a bunch of rabbits? Or if an animal hit an all-time high of bloodlust and had himself a feast?"

"Because that's not what happened," Lew responded coyly.

"Then what happened?" Vince asked, perturbed.

"We don't know."

"You don't know? Then how can you know it wasn't what I said?"

"Look around. Don't make me do your job for you."

"It's my day off. I'm not supposed to be doing *any* job today. I *should* be nursing my hangover and watching TV."

Lew stopped and put a hand on Vince's chest. Vince had to resist the urge to grab the grubby little mitt and twist it until it cracked. Lew saw the look and took his hand away quickly. "Look, I just want you to come to the same conclusion as me. On your own. Solidarity, my friend."

Vince heaved a massive, over-dramatic sigh and slightly nodded his head. He started to look at the scene with a discerning eye and he almost immediately saw it wasn't either of the scenarios he had offered previously.

"You got it," Lew said, knowing the shift in look his partner had.

"Yeah. If someone had decided to do a little backyard butcher job on these animals, they left a lot of viable meat behind. And that goes double for any predator that was looking for an early morning feast. This attack looks more frenzied…more needy and desperate."

Despite himself, Vince couldn't help but be intrigued by the scene before him. "My guess is it was a rabid animal that came across a burrow and the disease in its brain took over with no notion of what it actually needed."

"Could be. But, then again, the dismemberment is fairly clean. The torsos I would agree with you, could be from a rabid animal digging in, but the limbs and heads look as if they were twisted off and tossed aside. There's no ragged edge that would suggest a removal by teeth. No teeth marks on any of the limbs themselves either."

Lew's eyebrows curved upwards, waiting for Vince to ask his question.

"Okay, pal. What's your thought on what happened here?"

Lew shrugged his shoulders, trying to play off the question as best he could. "Oh, I don't know. Vampires? Werewolves? Satanists?" He gave a small chuckle.

"Be serious, Lew." Vince rolled his eyes and burped up a little acid.

Lew stopped walking and turned to Vince looking earnest for the first time since Vince had arrived. "You know me, partner. You know I don't like to put something into the universe until I am fairly certain I can prove it."

He looked around nervously and then stepped uncomfortably close to Vince. "The second I saw this…mess…I got a chill that didn't go away. It's still there."

He held up his arms to show Vince his goosebumps. "This feels almost ritualistic. The Satanist comment wasn't entirely a goofball one."

Vince glanced over his shoulder at the chaotic scene and shook his head. "Where are the symbols? Where's the order to indicate ritual? There's no order to *any* of this. There's no continuity."

"Everyone starts somewhere. Maybe they're new at it? Don't know exactly what they're doing?"

Lew scratched the back of his head and bit the inside of his lip. "I don't think it was a ritual in the strictest of terms, but more…" He trailed off and looked into the distance and Vince saw a fear in his partner's eyes he hadn't seen before. "Ceremonial, I guess. Sinister."

Vince stepped close to Lew and grabbed his arm gently. "I get that. And you're wise to sit on this until there's more evidence; something substantial to go on. I trust you and that gut of yours. Let's just take it a step at a time."

Lew stared back for a long moment and then patted Vince's slightly distended belly and smiled. "Not sure I'm the one with the gut."

The dark mood broke, and Vince shoved Lew away and shook his head.

There was a sudden commotion and both men turned toward the voice that was calling out urgently.

"Aronson? Monroe? Where are the detectives? I need them now!"

The voice came from a woman who staggered out from behind a small grove of trees. She was sheet white and looked as if she were about to pass out. Both men took a step toward her, and she locked eyes with them.

"Detectives. There's something you should see."

5

Detectives Aronson and Monroe, and Deputy Samuels walked through the small grove of trees that skirted the greater forest, none of them speaking. Samuels led the way, seemingly out of breath and hardly able to walk. They rounded a corner into a small clearing and the smell hit them; an odor like rotten meat, vomit, and boiled flesh had been stirred up and dropped into this small area. It took everything in Vince's power to keep his gorge from rising again. He looked to his partner, and saw he was in the same state of discomfort.

Their eyes wandered the scene, and it was somehow far worse than what they had already encountered. Whereas the clearing had mostly been filled with rabbits, here there was a whole variety of dismembered and eviscerated creatures: rabbits, rats, a couple foxes, something that looked like it was once a coyote, and a peafowl. The scene was gruesome, more red than green covered the ground and surrounding plant life. Deputy Samuels excused herself unceremoniously, leaving the Detectives to poke around.

Vince and Lew stood silently for nearly five minutes, trying to form an opinion of what could have possibly gone on here.

Lew grabbed Vince's arm and tilted his head. "You hear that?"

Vince cocked his head slightly and listened intently to try and pick up on whatever it was Lew had heard, but there was nothing. Then, a soft, small moan. "Yeah, I got it."

"Where's it coming from?" Lew sounded nearly out of breath.

Vince listened for another moment and then pointed to a small area near a crooked tree where the grass had grown knee-high. Lew unholstered his pistol and Vince followed. They both picked a path to flank the sound, while watching out for the abundance of blood and gore as best they could.

As they neared the moaning sound the smell worsened tenfold, and Vince wished he would have brought some peppermint oil with him. Then again, he hadn't a clue what he was walking into on his day off. The tops of the tall grass began to give way, revealing a semicircle of flattened grasses, and in the middle of this cleared out spot, leaning against the lone tree was a young man who appeared to be in his mid-twenties and under a great deal of duress. Vomit covered his clothes and on the ground around him, mixed in with the vomit, was blood.

Instinctively, Vince reached for his radio, but remembered once again that he shouldn't even be involved with this bit of lunacy. "Get on your walkie and get the paramedics out here. Now!"

Lew raised his radio to his lips and called for the paramedics, his full attention never wavering from the young man on the ground. When the call was complete, he held out a hand toward the bloodied man.

"Hey there. I am Detective Monroe. This here is Detective Aronson. Are you hurt? Do you need medical attention?"

The man continued to moan, but his eyes rolled up to take in the two detectives. After what seemed an eternity, he opened his mouth and spoke. "I threw up. I don't think my body is used to this food."

Vince glanced at Lew out of the corner of his eye. "He's delirious." Then he focused his attention back on the man on the ground.

"Sir, I'm thinking you're right about throwing up; looks like you did it a few times. But what I need to know right now is if you need medical attention. Are you injured? Were you attacked?"

The man rubbed his belly that looked unnaturally large and let forth a gigantic belch. Vince and Lew both covered their noses with the backs of their hands and involuntarily grunted, the air that forcefully entered the atmosphere was putrid, almost as if the man on the ground was rotting from the inside out.

"I threw up. I'm not used to this new diet," the man said again.

Lew knew he shouldn't speak on it until he was certain, but the bells of knowledge were ringing loud in his ears, so he said, "Bud, I'm fairly sure eating raw woodland creatures is not a diet any human could get used to if we're being honest with each other. And I'd like to think we are."

The man on the ground looked up at Lew, his bottom lip trembling, making him appear more like a small child who has a stomachache and doesn't know why. "I threw it all up. All of it. I don't feel so good."

And then he vomited again. But the vomit sort of trickled out of his mouth and intermingled were strands of dark red blood.

A rustling sound caused Vince and Lew to look behind them and they saw the paramedic crew approaching. They wore hazmat suits; the deputy had most likely warned them about the smell. Vince stepped to the side to let them pass. The lead medic looked at Vince. He appeared calm within his bubble.

"Dangerous?"

Vince shrugged.

"Doubt it. He keeps mumbling about not being able to keep his food down. I think he's in shock."

The paramedic nodded and stepped past, the hazmat suit impervious to the red and greyish-brown stains that were appearing as he walked.

"Good afternoon, sir. Can you tell me your name?"

Vince noticed the paramedic kept a little distance between himself and the man on the ground, just in case the man had a sudden urge to lunge.

"Can you tell me your name?" the paramedic repeated.

The man looked up at the paramedic pathetically and closed his eyes slowly. "I threw up."

The paramedic made a point to look all around, as if taking in the scene for the first time, before answering. "I can see that. I'm sorry to hear it. Do you know your name? Or where you are?"

The man furrowed his brow, deep in thought for a long moment. "I'm Martin. Pickney. I'm by the woods."

His demeanor changed again. "I threw up. I'm sorry. I didn't mean to. It's this new diet, you see."

The paramedic nodded sympathetically. "I understand. And there's nothing to be ashamed of. We all throw up sometimes. In fact, I saw *this* guy," and the paramedic jabbed a thumb in the direction of Vince, "throw up not too long ago. He wasn't ashamed at all. Is it okay if I take a look at you and make sure you aren't hurt? Do I have your permission to examine you?"

The man frowned deeply but nodded his head and went back to moaning.

The lead paramedic nodded to the woman that was with him and she moved to one side of Martin and began cleaning him up slowly and carefully while the lead began checking his vitals and poking and prodding him, asking him questions along the way.

Lew moved over next to Vince, and they conferred while the paramedics did their preliminaries. "I was thinking after he's gone to the hospital and is back to his normal self we should sit and have a chat with him."

Vince looked at Lew. "There are only animals here. No homicide."

"Usually starts with animals."

Lew looked down at Pickney and mused, "Could be a new drug. I think that would be worth checking into."

It took Vince a moment to realize his partner was absolutely right.

Why else would someone gorge themselves on animals to the point of vomiting. It really made no sense. But it *did* make sense if he was hopped up on something. New designer drugs were constantly being developed, and Vince prided himself on being in the know whenever a new one popped up. Maybe this one was so new that this guy had been running tests to see if it was viable. More likely, this was the lab rat that the manufacturer was *using* to test the new drug. Vince nodded his head.

"Makes sense to me. We'll have them run toxicology and test the vomit. Then we'll have a nice little chat and figure out what he's been putting in his veins."

"Or up his nose," Lew concluded, touching his nose and raising his eyebrows.

The lead paramedic stood up and approached Vince. "It doesn't appear that he has any contusions, and the blood seems to be from the animals. I heard you talking and bagged up a sample of the vomit. When we get him to the hospital, they'll run some labs; a whole gamut to see if he's on anything. Once the doctor deems him to be sound of mind, they will give you a call. You want restraints?"

"What's your rec?"

The paramedic shrugged. "Something isn't right here. I don't know if he's going to rile himself up at some point. For safety I would say restrain him until he's back in his own head."

Vince nodded and looked at Lew who also nodded. "Take him in, strap him down, and we will get to the bottom of why this fine young gentleman decided to go wild on a bunch of helpless animals."

It was the paramedic's turn to nod. "I'll tell you one thing. I do not envy the bowel movements he's going to have to endure trying to process everything he ate. I would rather have food poisoning."

And then as an afterthought, "He might have that too anyhow."

The paramedic turned back to Martin to prepare him for transport. "Okay Martin, we're going to go on a little ride. You up for it?"

Lew clapped Vince on the shoulder and smiled at him. "Well, buddy, why don't you go enjoy the rest of your day off and I will see you tomorrow."

Vince looked back without amusement. They both knew there was no way either of them was going home to rest until they had a chance to talk to Mr. Pickney. "I *am* hungry."

Lew screwed up his nose in disgust, as if to say there was no way he could have an appetite, but he nodded anyway, and they left the paramedics to their work.

6

The burger Vince got was just greasy enough to let him know he would need some antacids, or he would be up all night with intense heartburn. It did, however, quell the turmoil that had afflicted him up until this point in the day. And with a new case opening, he had little time for his hangover anyhow.

Across from him Lew tucked away an extra-large portion of breakfast foods. He had already downed two eggs over-easy, two pieces of toast, three meaty slabs of bacon, and a half stack of thick pancakes. Now he was working his way through a Belgian waffle that smelled like it was cooked in bacon grease, which it most likely was.

"I don't know how you eat all that crap without gaining a single pound. You must have the metabolism of a hummingbird." Vince never got used to how much food Lew could pack away.

Lew responded through a mouthful of waffle, "Metabolism, my good man, is definitely a piece of the puzzle. That and a shit ton of exercise."

He jabbed his fork at Vince, splattering syrup across the table in the process. "You should really try it sometime. Might do you some good. You paunch anymore and I'm gonna have to name the damn thing."

Vince never minded the little shots his partner threw his way. He knew why he was overweight and couldn't drop the pounds. Everyone has their little vices. Vince's main squeeze was the bottle. If he were offered the opportunity to drink, he would drink. The only time he really felt ashamed of this fact was when he stared at the bottom of an empty glass bottle that he started earlier in the day. Most people in town gossiped it had to do with his divorce, which they assumed had been a nasty affair. Vince had to relinquish everything else in order to keep his little cabin. But truth be told, Vince's drinking had started in his early twenties; he just knew how to hide it better back then. He would chock it up to living his best life in his twenties, and no one questioned him, because he was doing fine work as a policeman. And no one really asked him now because he was doing fine work as a detective. Lew asked him on occasion about it, but never prodded too far.

"I will tell you something, though, Vince. If I keep eating here, Lauren," he raised his voice when he said her name, "is going to have to roll me outta here one of these days."

Lauren's head peeked out above the cook's station, and she smiled. Vince imagined she had a little crush on the good Detective Lewis Monroe, but he couldn't really blame her.

Of all the men who resided in the tri-cities, which amounted to nearly 3,000, Detective Lewis Monroe would stand out above most if not all of them. Sure, he had the looks going for him, but he also had charisma and could charm most anyone he met when he was trying. That combination played a large factor in why he was such a good interrogator.

Vince remembered one time they were questioning a kid in his twenties about a theft at the local mall. They were getting nowhere fast, and time was running out before they would be forced to release him back into the wild. When there is only circumstantial evidence at best the clock doth tick. It didn't matter that they basically had him dead to rights, they simply didn't have the proof they needed. Vince was flustered and had run out of tactics; Lew was heading that direction. So, Lew had decided there was nothing left to lose, except their main suspect, and he walked into the interrogation room, looked the young man square in the face, smiled his biggest come-hither smile, and said, "Come on, buddy. It's not that big a deal." And just like that, the kid cracked and confessed. Lew had exited the room with a beaming smile and had reached up and closed Vince's mouth that was hanging agape in shock.

The trust in each other's instincts grew exponentially after that case. If one of them had a hunch they both followed it to either solve the case or find a dead end they could eliminate. Most of the time the hunches solved the case, but every once in a while, they hit a dead end. Such was the case with EZ Does It. But they weren't averse to sheer dumb luck either.

Any good team of detectives would say their success is predicated on trust, instinct, hard work, and a heaping helping of luck. Fortunately, Vince and Lew hadn't needed to utilize their reservoir of luck very often.

Lew finally broke the silence, having mopped up the syrup from his plate with a piece of toast he had somehow acquired in the last five minutes. "So, what the hell was that out by the forest today? I've never seen anything like it. Nothing close to anything like it."

Vince shook his head. He was just as befuddled as his partner. "I don't really know. I didn't even know we had that many animals living in the forest. How do you even clean up something like that?"

"Let the dogs at it. They'll have it licked clean in no time."

Vince made a face. "I guess. Makes sense."

"Course it does. Now, how do we want to do this?" Lew wiped his hands off with a napkin and belched a little too loudly. "That's sitting nice."

"I figure once the officer stationed outside Mr. Pickney's room informs us he's ready to be questioned, we have the interrogation room ready and comfortable."

Lew screwed up his face and shook his head. "You don't think he'll clam up? Right now, all he can be accused of is eating a bunch of raw animals. As far as I know there is nothing within that that makes him a criminal. What if we take a walk with him? We could meet him at the hospital, be the good guys who release him from those nasty restraints and walk him out of the hospital. Just three friendly chums having a chat as we walk back out into the wide world."

"That could work. It would definitely put him more at ease and maybe make him less embarrassed by his morning feast."

Vince nodded his head, agreeing with his partner. His mind flashed through the possibilities of what could have possessed the man to do what he did so he would be better prepared for anything that came about during the conversation. His mind kept coming back to drugs, but there was an itch in the back of his brain that told him this had nothing to do with drugs.

As if on cue, his cell phone twittered, indicating a text message. Almost simultaneously, Lew's cell phone let out a low blast, like a trombone being blown to its limit. They both looked at their phones and read the same text:

> Pathology is back. No drugs present in Mr. Pickney's bloodstream. No trace amounts of anything. There was an abnormality in the panels we took, but it definitely isn't drug related. We will investigate further to try and find out the anomaly. Give the guy another hour or so and he will be ready for release. We want to monitor him for a while longer to ensure he doesn't have food poisoning, but he hasn't thrown up since he arrived at the hospital and appears to be resting comfortably, so we aren't too concerned about food poisoning at this point. Will inform you on test results of the bloodwork after the panels have been run.

They put their cell phones away and looked at each other. Vince chewed the inside of his lip and Lew ran his tongue over his teeth.

Both were trying to make sense of the *blood abnormality* that might be present.

Lew spoke first. "I like our new drug thought. Something that's too new to be recognized maybe."

"Maybe. The drug angle makes sense. But something is bugging me about it. It's not sitting in my head quite right." Lew was nodding while Vince was talking. The fact that both of them agreed something was slightly off gave them more confidence in the intuition.

Lew stood up, throwing his napkin onto the table. "I've got to go see a man about a piss. When I come back, we should head on over to the hospital. Have our little chat with Mr. Martin Pickney. I have a feeling we will have this thing wrapped up in time for me to take you out for a nice steak dinner."

Vince smiled at this. "I do declare you are trying to seduce me, Mr. Monroe."

Lew pointed at him and replied, "That's Detective Monroe."

And then his face became serious. "What if it's some sort of brain disease? What if the blood abnormality is related to something like dementia? He didn't really know what he was doing because his brain isn't completing the cycle."

"That's a good thought. I'll text the pathologist back while you take one for the team. I got lunch. I'll see you outside in three."

Vince stood up and stretched, feeling his bones creak and groan. He thought that maybe it *was* time for him to look into eating better and exercising a bit more.

He left money on the table and Lew disappeared around the corner into the bathroom. The slight tug on his brain still bothered him, but he didn't know what possible reason there could be for the feeling. Two options: New designer drug or brain disease. Both options made a lot of sense; but neither one fit in the holes quite right.

He walked past Lauren, raising a hand in a goodbye, and stepped out into the late afternoon September heat. Vince had the feeling the steak dinner he had been promised was going to have to wait a bit longer.

7

Lew and Vince pulled up to the state hospital a half hour later and parked as far away from the entrance as possible. Both had been fairly silent on the ride over as each ran scenarios in their heads. Neither would admit it, but they were uneasy about the conversation they were about to have with Mr. Pickney. Trepidation was not a natural occurrence with either of them, but neither of them took the initiative to exit the vehicle.

The car idled and Vince and Lew breathed evenly, waiting for the other to move first. Finally, Lew turned the vehicle off, and Vince unbuckled his seat belt. Yet they still did not head toward the hospital. Inside the car the two men sat, allowing the tension to build until it was almost unbearable.

Just as it seemed Lew might return his key to the ignition and simply drive back to the precinct, he laughed out a small barking laugh. "What the hell is going on here, partner?"

Vince knew what Lew was talking about, but he was in stall mode. "What do you mean?"

"I think you know. This…hesitation. We don't hesitate. We aren't unsure of ourselves."

"True."

"So why are we today?"

"Dunno. I think maybe there's something more to this than we originally thought. I think it goes beyond drugs or brain disease. I think it might be something we aren't prepared for, and we're scared because of it."

Vince shook his head, trying to loosen himself from the feeling. It didn't work. If anything, it dug in deeper.

Lew swallowed, hearing his throat click, feeling the dryness there. "Yeah. I don't know what it is, but I've started thinking about drafting a will."

Vince wasn't quite sure why he found this amusing, but he began to chuckle, which unzipped a lot of the tension, allowing them both to breathe. Soon, Vince and Lew were laughing until they felt tears brimming in their eyes. Once they composed themselves, they knew it was time to move. It was time to go have a little chat with Mr. Pickney.

Lew put a calming hand on Vince's arm and nodded slightly, "We are a good team. I know that; you know that; hell, everyone in the tri-cities knows that. As long as we treat this like any other case we have had, we'll be fine."

Vince patted Lew's hand and nodded slightly. "That we are, partner. Almost as close as lovers we."

Lew pushed Vince away and they both laughed again. Then they exited the car to head into the hospital.

8

Vince didn't know what to expect as they entered the hospital lobby, but serene was not one of the top five on the board. It seemed that no one decided to be injured or sick today. There was nobody in the waiting room, and the nurses and technicians all appeared to be whispering to each other, almost as if they thought if they raised their voices the injured and sick people would hear them and come running. There was no chaos, no codes, no drama. It was almost like being in a library and Vince had the sudden urge to walk up to reception and ask where he could find a book on brain disease. He stifled a smile at the thought.

The men approached the desk and Lew showed his badge and asked where Mr. Pickney was being held against his will. The desk nurse frowned at the joke but gave them the room number and a vague description of how to get there. She pressed a button, and they heard a click and pushed on the now unlocked door to enter the hospital proper.

After a few twists and turns Vince felt as though they might have gotten turned around somewhere, but then they saw Dr. Victoria Stansbrough. She raised a finger to indicate they should wait for her for a moment and then went back to conversing with a nurse. Vince shifted from foot to foot, impatient to get this interview going. He felt the longer he waited the less nerve he would have to follow through on the whole process. He glanced over at his partner and got the same sense from him.

Finally, Dr. Stansbrough walked over and nodded her head. "Gentlemen, I do think you have come to the hospital on an historic day. I don't remember this place ever being this quiet. I guess that's a good thing. We can keep the gossip between staff regarding the curious case of Martin Pickney, animal gobbler."

Lew let out a nearly silent chuckle and then said, "See, this is why I like you Doc. That curmudgeon of a nurse you got out front couldn't take a joke. It wasn't even at her expense, but she scowled at me like I told a dirty joke in church."

"Yeah. Well, she's retiring next week. You didn't hear it from me, but a lot of the other nurses call her Nurse Stickup."

She smiled conspiratorially. "If you catch my meaning."

Both men nodded and then Vince said, "Listen, we were talking about our friend before we got here. Is there any possibility that he might have some sort of brain disease that could cause him to suddenly get hungry for raw animal innards? I know you ruled out drugs, so it's the only other avenue we could rationalize. That, or it's a new street drug that uses compounds that aren't found on any drug screening."

Dr. Stansbrough frowned, deep in thought. "I guess we *could* do a CT or MRI to try and rule out the possibility. We didn't think of it because he appeared to have no head trauma. He answered our cognitive suite of questions with flying colors; he was just a little fuzzy on the events of the last twelve hours or so, which, considering the circumstances I don't blame the guy. As for a new drug it would have to be an entirely new compound using nothing that has been used before. Even something that's unknown will usually cause a spike somewhere that's out of the ordinary."

"You said there was a blood abnormality. Could that be an effect of drug use?" Lew piped in.

"It's possible, but unlikely. Unless this improbable new designer drug mutates the blood cells. New studies have shown that consistent drug use can alter the actual genetic structure within a human being.

You know how they say that addictions can be passed down from generation to generation?"

"Sins of the father," Lew offered.

"In a way. Well, these studies have shown that the actual addiction can imprint on a person's DNA, altering the genetics to have a greater weakness toward addiction, which can be passed on to future generations.

"Intense trauma can have an effect like that as well. You know how someone can experience something wholly awful and not remember a second of it after the fact? That is possibly when an imprint is made in the DNA. The body literally tells itself to forget the event and redacts the information. The problem with *that* theory in connection with what's happening inside the young man you are here to see is that something appears to have imprinted on his actual blood cells. They have been altered, but he seems to be functioning perfectly fine. There doesn't appear to be any side effects with regards to that mutation."

Dr. Stansbrough shook her head. "We are sending some of the samples off to a national institute that deals specifically with blood cells. Our hope is they will be able to offer us a little insight into what exactly is happening within Mr. Pickney."

Lew couldn't help himself. He grinned and asked the question Vince had been hoping he wouldn't ask. "Are you saying our boy here could develop superpowers?"

Dr. Stansbrough surprised them both by laughing. "Nothing like that. No. He's not going to gain telekinesis all of a sudden. Fairy tales are still fairy tales."

Vince looked over at Lew and saw the disappointment written all over his face. He decided to take over for a moment. "Is there any way to test his DNA to see if it has been imprinted?"

"Not really. It's still just theoretical. There *is* a strong enough basis to go off of for the scientific community to investigate, but nothing has been proven yet."

Then as an afterthought, "I guess you could describe an imprint on DNA as akin to having a scar on your body after your wound heals."

Vince was starting to grasp the complexity of what Dr. Stansbrough was saying, and agreed that this case was not tied into any sort of imprinting of the DNA. Still the mutated blood cells were concerning. He made a mental note to follow up on the test results as soon as they were available.

"I guess we better go see our curious case, huh?" Vince rubbed his hands together and clapped them softly.

"Yes. Let's walk that way and I'll get his discharge papers in order."

Dr. Stansbrough led the way toward Martin Pickney's room. As they approached the nurse's station, she tilted her head slightly toward them. "You know there's a theory that the Atlanteans messed around with genetics, purposefully imprinting DNA."

"Atlanteans?" Lew queried. "You mean the people from Atlantis? We're starting to sound like a Marvel movie."

"Why would anyone do that?" Vince asked, reentering the conversation.

"No clue whatsoever. But it would be fascinating to find out if it were true."

Dr. Stansbrough talked to one of the nurses and grabbed a stack of paperwork. "All right, let's go remove his I.V. and he's all yours."

"I.V.?" Vince asked, raising his eyebrows.

"We had to pump him full of fluids to try and counteract any food poisoning he might have acquired from eating his meal of critter tartare."

Vince nodded and then the two detectives followed her into Room 157.

Martin Pickney was lying in the bed, his eyes wide open, gently tugging at the restraints. His eyes flicked over to Vince and Lew, and he tried to shrink himself down to get away from them.

"Hey, can anyone tell me why I'm in restraints? I didn't do anything wrong." His voice was noncombative, almost apologetic.

Lew took the lead, throwing on a brilliant smile to try and put the man at ease. "Mr. Pickney, nobody believes you did anything wrong. The only reason we put you in restraints is because you seemed confused when we found you and we didn't want you to accidentally hurt yourself."

He gestured around the room to Vince and Dr. Stansbrough. "But I think we all can agree that you are in a much better state of mind and have no intention of hurting yourself, so just as soon as the I.V. is removed from your arm, we'll get those restraints off you and take you home."

Martin visibly relaxed a little, but he still seemed a bit on edge.

"By the bye, do you happen to remember anything from the last 24 hours? Or where we found you?" Lew had almost already charmed the man. Another few minutes and he would probably buy both the detectives a steak dinner, no further questions your honor.

"I was outside the forest in Angel's Rest." Lew had already lowered the man's defenses and was talking to him like they were old friends.

"That's right. What were you doin' out there? You know there are bears in those woods?" Lew came dangerously close to chucking Martin in the shoulder but refrained.

"I...I wasn't aware. I think I was going to see some friends. They told me about a series of paths through the forest that led from Angel's Rest to Perdition."

Lew chuckled lightly and shook his head. "Man, the names of the places out here."

He lapsed into momentary silence and then looked directly at Martin. "Hey, why didn't you just drive over there?"

Martin looked down for a moment. "The drive is about thirty or forty miles from Angel's Rest to Perdition. But if you cut through the forest, it's only about a three-mile walk." He looked back up at Lew.

"That's right." Lew nodded his head, as if remembering something important. "Because it's a national—" He let his voice trail off so Martin could pick up the sentence.

"Preserve. Yeah. No roads through the forest."

This is where Lew shined brightest. He knew how to involve someone in a conversation until they were so invested, they ended up doing most of the talking. Let them answer the questions or open-ended sentences so they thought they were the ones coming up with all the answers. And Vince loved to sit back and watch it unfold. It was like watching a street magician.

"A Preserve. Yes. I'm glad they still have those around. We don't want to destroy all of nature, right?" Lew chuckled. Martin copied the laugh.

"We humans and our industry. That was the other reason I wanted to walk. There are too many emissions in the environment, too much pollution. We gotta watch our...what's it called. Shoot..." Martin trailed off, trying to remember the correct term.

Lew got him smoothly back on track. "Carbon footprint?"

Martin snapped his fingers, reminding everyone in the room he was still in restraints. "That's the one. We gotta watch our carbon footprint."

Vince looked over at Dr. Stansbrough, who stood transfixed by the interaction. The look said that she had been trying to get answers out of this young man and hadn't gotten anywhere, and now Lew had walked in and within three minutes had opened him up like a can of worms. It truly was mesmerizing, and Vince noticed the good doctor had stopped with her hands in mid-air on their way to remove the I.V. because she was completely locked in on the conversation.

Vince cleared his throat. "We're going to get this I.V. out of you, Mr. Pickney and then you will be a free man."

Dr. Stansbrough flinched, and then remembered herself quickly. Within seconds the I.V. was out, and Lew was carefully removing the restraints with great big ripping sounds as the Velcro gave up. When they were off Martin rubbed his arms to get the circulation going again.

Vince thanked the doctor and then turned to Martin. "You wanna do a bit more walking? We would love to find out what happened last night and maybe fill in some details that might be missing for you. Sound good?"

"Sure. I'm just ready to get out of here. And my stomach feels like I ate a whole helping of lead balls."

Lew and Vince glanced at each other but didn't say a word.

Martin went into the bathroom to change out of his hospital gown and when he came back out, he appeared halfway to normal. Nobody would look at him and think that this guy had eaten a smorgasbord of small animals no more than 24 hours ago.

9

When they reached the sidewalk in front of the hospital, Martin inhaled deeply through his nose. Vince and Lew looked at him, hoping he wasn't about to do anything crazy.

Martin offered them a shy smile and said, "Smells like medicine in there. And death. The air's better out here."

Lew nodded his head in understanding. The left side of Vince's mouth moved slightly upward into a smile.

"So, where can we take you, Mr. Pickney?" Lew asked, rubbing his hands together and stretching his back.

Martin looked at Lew, surprised. "I'm not going down to the station?"

Lew stopped and looked earnestly at Martin for a moment. "Do you *want* to go down to the station?"

"I mean, I thought that's why you guys picked me up from the hospital." A confused look was spreading across Martin's face.

Vince clapped him on the shoulder and said, "There is nothing you did out in the woods, as far as we're aware, that would make us take you into custody."

"You kind of did go a little crazy on some animals, but none of the animals you gorged on were protected, so there's no need for that," Lew chimed in.

Martin's look turned from confusion to shame and color slowly crept up into his face. "Yeah, I don't really remember that. I just remember throwing up a lot and then I was in the hospital."

"Maybe you had a bit too much fun last night. Drink a little drink, smoke a little dope perhaps. The night could get away from you easy, but I gotta tell you, that is one hell of a way to satisfy the munchies."

There was no accusation in Lew's tone. He was simply trying to gauge Martin's reaction.

Martin shook his head. "No. That was waiting for me on the other side of the forest, but something tells me I didn't quite make it all the way through."

He caught himself. "I mean, weed is legal here, right? I'm not going to go in on some stupid little charge for marijuana. I'm just assuming my friends had it waiting."

Martin would have continued his blubbering if Lew hadn't set a hand gently onto his shoulder. Martin flinched ever so slightly at the touch. "Nah. Don't worry about all that. I've done it a time or two myself. Helps calm my nerves. What about any harder drugs? Did you ever try that EZ Does It shit when it was around?"

Lew was probing, but the way he probed was very congenial and friendly. Nonetheless, Martin had now begun to fidget.

"I mean, I did ecstasy once. But just one time. Too out of my own head. I didn't like it. But I don't really do drugs. Just a little weed every now and again." And then as an afterthought, "Same as you."

The first alarm bell began to ring in Vince's head. He couldn't pinpoint why the alarm was sounding off, but he knew it had to do with Martin recalling Lew's previous statement. Up until this point he had been quite confused and demure, but the cognizance to cover himself hinted that maybe Martin wasn't quite as confused as he let on.

Then again, he could be returning to his normal self, and he was an astute person in everyday life. But Vince logged it away in case more came up that compounded the interest of how clever this guy could be. Either way, it seemed like Martin was feeling a little more comfortable in their presence.

Lew broke the silence with a quick snort. "Same as me. I hear that.

Listen, don't worry about the ecstasy. Especially since it was a one-time deal. I just want to make sure there is nothing new out and about that we should be worried about."

When Vince and Lew first became partners, Vince always got terribly upset when Lew let the person they were questioning know so many details regarding why they were having a conversation. He would tell a murderer about a murder weapon they had found, or a drug dealer about the extra bit of stash they had found that had been tucked away by one of his lackeys.

He remembered one conversation in particular where they had a suspected serial killer sitting in front of them in the interrogation room. At the crime scene they had found what appeared to be the murder weapon; a piece of piano wire strung between two wooden dowels. Lew had told the suspect that they had found the murder weapon; fishing line strung between two metal rods. Vince didn't notice the discrepancy at the time, because he was appalled at the information he was handing out freely.

Vince pulled him out of the interrogation room and was about to lay into him when he saw the bird-who-ate-the-canary grin on his face. Lew explained that serial killers often had very vain tendencies. They were quite particular about the how and the why and the where of their murders. He explained how deep down most serial killers want to get caught, so they left sloppy little mistakes that would add up until the evidence was overwhelming and there was nothing left to do but slap on the cuffs and haul them away. If you insult their intelligence or cheapen the experience for them, they usually had a tell, like in poker. And their little suspect had told Lew that he was the killer. Now all they had to do was secure enough evidence to convict him, which they did within a week.

Psychology had never been one of Vince's strong suits, so he was still very confused, because the guy sitting in the interrogation room hadn't said anything at all when Lew mentioned the fishing line. Lew tapped his own forehead and smiled at Vince, telling him that as soon as he made the error on the weapon of choice a giant vein had popped out on the guy's forehead. He had been trying so hard not to give himself away that he had done so in spectacular fashion. Lew was incredibly pleased with himself, and Vince had to admit that he was quite impressed.

So now, when Lew took these leaps of truth with a possible suspect, he no longer questioned it. He just sat back and watched the criminals incriminate themselves.

Lew had been going on about their case involving EZ Does It and he was winding up saying, "Here's the thing Martin. If there *is* a new drug out there that causes people to gobble up little critters, we need to know about it. It's not only a danger to our wildlife population, but people can die from ingesting raw meat."

Martin shrugged his shoulders. "I don't know about all that, but I can assure you I haven't been taking any drugs. I haven't really been around anyone who could have slipped me anything anyhow."

Lew nodded pensively. "Do you work in the area?"

"I work at one of the gas stations in Angel's Rest. Nothing glamorous, but it pays the few bills I have."

Lew turned to Vince and said, "Hey, didn't we bust a small drug ring at one of the Gas 'n Go's a while back?"

Vince nodded his head. "Yeah, the one right off the Interstate. Angel's Rest. Regular old cocaine if I remember correctly."

"No, I work at the Pump 'n Shop. I've never worked at a Gas 'n Go." Martin made sure he was extra clear on this point.

Lew laughed and clapped Martin on the back. "No worries. Just had a moment of nostalgia."

He gestured in front of them. "Our chariot awaits. How about we get you home? Whaddya say, Marty?"

Martin returned to his demure state and mumbled, "Sounds good. I'll give you directions."

Lew paused at the driver's side door and looked over at Vince and winked. "That sounds like a damn fine plan to me. Let's get on, shall we?"

They all piled into the car and were on the main road in less than a minute. In less than ten minutes they pulled onto the street where Martin lived. Three minutes later they had deposited their package on the front porch of his tiny home, one of those deals with the wheels so you could move your house around if you wanted. Five minutes later Vince and Lew were heading back to the precinct. The alarm bell still rang in Vince's head, but the volume had been turned down for now. Both Vince and Lew hoped that was the last they would hear from Mr. Martin Pickney.

10

Vince and Lew pulled up to the police precinct and Lew slid his dark grey Cadillac into a spot close to the door in the covered garage. They stepped out and involuntarily stretched, as if tempting the day to slough off onto the ground.

As soon as they entered the building the sounds of ringing telephones and the clack of keyboards could be heard. This was the busiest precinct in the Tri-Cities, and it was the oldest. Central precinct stood where the original wooden shack had been in the early 1900s. In fact, the building had not been updated until the turn of the century. And they almost kept it as an historic site, but the vote did not go the way of the preservationists. So, the small, decrepit shack that had a single main room with three jail cells had been bulldozed to make way for the multi-level precinct that stood in its place now.

Vince and Lew wound their way through intake and mug shots and booked it straight for the darkened rear section of the floor. This was where their office was, along with the call center and a smattering of police officers who needed the ambient noise, at least that's what *they* referred to it as, in order to concentrate. Vince was fairly convinced they were the officers who didn't appreciate human contact and avoided it as much as possible. A couple of the officers were even notorious for asking for assignments where they would be less likely to have to interact with the general public.

The detectives walked into their office, not expecting the chief of police and a representative from HR to greet them. Lew nearly jumped back out of the open door before putting a hand to his heart and letting out a relieved *whoosh* of air.

"How about you warn a fella next time, Chief?" Lew laughed and the Chief allowed himself an unamused tilt of his lips.

The HR rep sat in the darkest section of the office, causing Vince to turn on every light in the room to check for any more hidden surprises. As far as he could tell, the only surprise left was why HR was there in the first place.

The Chief waited until the men settled behind their desks. Lew pulled out an oft-chewed-on cigar that he never lit. He had informed Vince that he liked the flavor and the small amount of nicotine that made it into his system helped him focus and catch criminals. Vince didn't have to smell the smoke, so he didn't mind. The Chief didn't seem to take notice, but the HR rep went sheet white. Lew saw his face and quickly tucked the cigar back into his desk drawer.

"I don't light it. I just like to chew on it. Is that against regulations?"

Lew was rapid-fire, not allowing the rep to get a word in edgewise. Another tactic he had picked up throughout the years. And now Vince waited for the closer that would put the issue to bed before it was even brought up.

"You know what, I'll read through the rule book and make sure I'm not doing anything I shouldn't. No need to concern yourself over it. Now, what are you fine gentlemen doing down here in the doldrums?"

The Chief shifted in his chair, which creaked and groaned, making Vince thank the gods the Chief wasn't a jolly, fat man. He would have made splinters of the chair if he didn't weigh around a buck thirty soaking wet. A smile tried to worm its way onto Vince's lips, but he suppressed it and instead focused all his energy on what the Chief was about to say.

"You both know that I appreciate all you do for this department. You are the best detectives I have ever worked with, and everyone knows my stance on that matter."

Lew had begun to giggle. The Chief tried to ignore him. "However, there is a matter we need to discuss regarding discretion of verbiage that is used around others in the building that don't need to know the extent of whatever you are investigating."

Lew had his hand over his mouth, but the laughter seeped around the edges, causing the chuckle to take on a distinctive fart noise sound. This made Lew lose it completely, and he guffawed for a good few seconds while the Chief's coloring went from pale to deep red.

Finally, the Chief reached out and slammed his hand on Lew's desk, which was loud enough to cause a few heads in the bullpen to turn and gawk. "And just what the hell is so funny, Detective?"

Lew was desperately trying to get himself under control but was losing the battle. He shook his head and waved his hand trying to convey that nothing was funny actually, please continue with the reprimand.

The Chief leaned back in his seat and eyed Lew without humor. "No, I would really like to know what exactly set you off, son. So, we will wait until you get yourself under control, and then we will have our conversation."

The HR rep looked incredibly uncomfortable, and Vince simply sat at his desk silently, waiting for the laughter from Lew to abate. It took nearly three minutes for peace to be restored in the room. The Chief raised his eyebrows, seemingly undaunted in his need to know what humorous bit of information had found its way into Lew's brain.

"Chief, it's just..." Lew exhaled, feeling the last of the giggles being breathed away in the process. "You come in here with HR and all I can think of is every TV show and movie I've ever seen where the Chief tells the detectives to turn in their badge and gun because they are suspended. And I thought that cliché was too funny for whatever this is."

The Chief looked away for an instant, but it was long enough to one-eighty Lew's attitude. "Like hell you're here to suspend us."

There was a brief pause, and then the HR rep spoke up for the first time. "No *us*. Just *you*."

"You are on a paid leave from the department for the next two weeks. We have been approached by multiple witnesses who can attest to some of the tasteless jokes you have thrown around recently. The similarities in their accounts are too damning to simply slap your wrist and call it a day." The Chief suddenly looked very weary.

"Aren't you going to tell me what jokes I supposedly told to get the bum rush like this?" Lew didn't lose his temper often, but when he did, he bit like a viper. More often than not he ended up saying things that made the situation far worse. Vince was trying to will him to keep his mouth shut.

The HR rep leaned forward with a small folder and handed it to Lew, who yanked it out of his hands, looking disdainfully at the man. Lew rifled through the pages, taking no care to keep the papers attached to the staple that held them together. Then, to everyone's great surprise, Lew started laughing. Not a bitter, this is ridiculous, kind of laugh, but a wholehearted, entertained by himself, kind of laugh.

"Really, Chief? These are the jokes? These are pussycat jokes. Harmless."

"Not to some, Lew. The day and age we live in people are sensitive. You are exceptionally good at reading a room, but sometimes I think you feel you are at home when you are here, so you let your discretion slide around a bit. I pushed to get you the two weeks paid, so don't make me look bad."

Lew nodded his head, some of the incredulity returning to his face. "You pushed. It's not like you're the Chief of Police or anything. I don't know who you're pushing to make this happen."

Lew stared down the Chief for a few seconds before continuing, "All right, fine. You've been good to me, Chief. I'll do you this kindness."

The Chief rolled his eyes and then leaned forward, making sure Lew was paying special attention to what he was about to say. "And if I hear you've been in this building during your two-week furlough, I will take away the paid bit of your suspension. Stay home. Get rest. Read a book. I don't care what you do as long as you do it away from here."

Lew chewed the inside of his cheek and then gave a single, curt nod. "When do you want me gone?"

The Chief glanced at the clock on the wall. "Thirty minutes. Not a second longer."

He and the HR rep stood and walked out before Lew could even get in a single jab, which was probably for the best according to Vince's estimation.

As soon as they departed Vince held out his hand for the packet. Lew handed it over and Vince perused it, his mouth turning up every few seconds in the hint of a smile.

"See? You think it's funny." Lew motioned at the information. "I mean, you heard about that priest or whatever who was hired by that family to exorcise some demon out of their house and then he ended up holding the family at knife point until the cops came and dragged him off to the loony bin. Read that part." Lew waited.

"Paranormal investigator. But, yeah, I mean I get the joke, but whatever. You get a vacation. I would take it without complaint."

Vince handed the stack of papers back to Lew. "I have a feeling the Chief did right by you. I bet people were calling for you to be fired."

"Edward. That little dip wad. He's definitely one of the ones who ratted." Lew threw his hands up into the air in surrender. "Forget it. I'm going to go home and get some sleep and binge some shows and I'm going to do it right now."

Lew stood up from his desk, grabbed his pre-chewed cigar and a couple other personal items and walked out the door without another word. Vince was left alone in the quiet office, hoping nothing big would emerge while Lew was out of commission.

And then Vince remembered that he didn't have a car to take him home, so he stood abruptly and rushed out of the office, hoping to catch up to Lew before he left a burnt rubber trail on the pavement outside of the precinct.

11

Vince sat in front of his TV, staring through the screen and catching glimpses of individual pixels of red, green, and blue. The microwave brayed its alarm, pulling him from his reverie. Yet, he remained seated for a few more minutes, trying to gather his thoughts about the day he had.

The obvious pieces fell away as he tried to coerce the shades to the surface. The facts were thus: they had found a young guy surrounded by animal carcasses, which he had feasted on some time in the night. That man, Martin, had hardly remembered his meal or how he got to be outside of the forest. There had been no ritualistic imagery to suggest any cult proceedings.

The nuances tugged at Vince's mind, pulling him into the thin space that a detective held for ideas that straddled the line between intuition and paranoia. He had thought he glimpsed a few times where Martin had evaded, using his memory loss excuse as a way to weasel through a response without actually answering the question. There was a flicker in Martin's eyes that hinted at more knowledge than he was letting on. This was not encouraging. Usually if someone were being shifty once, there would be a repeat of some sort not too far down the line.

Now his partner was relegated to the sidelines and this rising sense of tension loomed large. Vince hoped it wouldn't snap before Lew came back. This foreboding lay heavily on him like a wool blanket; heavy and itchy.

Early in his career Vince would have shaken all thoughts of conspiracies out of his head, but he had been at this long enough to learn to trust his gut. He knew there was more to the case than what had been exposed earlier in the day. Unfortunately, there was nothing he could do about it unless it happened again.

The microwave beeped impatiently, and Vince stood up out of his recliner and made his way to the kitchen where his TV dinner would most likely be simultaneously boiling hot and still frozen. He removed the plastic carton, burning his fingers, and ripped the plastic off the top allowing the steam to rise into his face. The prison yard equivalent of Salisbury steak and smashed potatoes stared up at him. As unappetizing as it looked, Vince threw himself into the meal with great gusto finishing it in as many minutes as it took him to heat it.

Returning to his chair with a half empty bottle of Jamison and a glass, he settled in and began his nightly routine, which he referred to as the pour and gulp. Soon, he would be on the other side of the rainbow, dreaming dark dreams and hoping the sunlight wouldn't bring about the needle-like pain behind his eyes.

He was three glasses in when he passed out in his chair. And that is when the dreams came.

12

He was standing in front of the giant copse of trees that constituted Angel's Rest Forest. It was night. There were no sounds. Not a single bird chirped, no crickets played their leg music, and not even a ground creature stirred.

Vince felt the hair on the back of his neck rise, and he knew something unnatural was occurring. But he didn't know where to look to find it. That feeling of situational blindness was one of a Detective's worst nightmares. There was a distinct impotence involved when the room couldn't be read, and everyone was looking at you to solve the crime. This is how Vince felt.

Then a rustling in the underbrush near the edge of the forest. Instinctively, Vince reached for his gun, but he was in his flannel pajamas. So, he took a step back and watched for something, anything to emerge from the trees.

He didn't have to wait long. Without warning, Martin appeared and smiled at Vince. He put a finger to his lips and motioned for Vince to follow him into the forest.

Vince could feel the sweat standing out on his forehead and he had a surreal moment where he wondered if this was actually a dream, or if he was somehow standing in front of the forest. Before he could stop himself, his feet carried him toward the woods, his eyes straining to keep Martin in view.

He crossed the threshold and noted how much warmer it became.

After a few minutes of walking Martin turned to him, made the shushing motion once again and then stepped through a dense patch of bushes.

Vince hesitated for a moment, but then took a deep breath and followed. His footing almost failed as he entered a clearing and saw a mountain of dead animals in front of him. There were many more than the number he had seen earlier, and all of their eyes seemed to be staring directly at him.

Martin stood next to the pile, which towered over his head, and beckoned for Vince to join him, implying he wanted him to go ahead and give it a try. *Don't knock it 'til you try it*, rushed through Vince's head and for a brief moment he considered actually walking up to the pile, finding a small animal within and taking a bite. Just one little bite to see what all the fuss was about.

And then he was at the pile, and his hand was reaching out. The disconnected nature of the dream yanked the lucidity from Vince violently, but instead of waking up Vince was treated to a third-person view of what was happening.

He watched himself reach elbow deep into the pile, rummaging for something. The wet, squishing sounds of guts filled the clearing and then Vince had a small rabbit in his hands. He looked over at Martin for some sort of confirmation and when Martin smiled and nodded, he bent over the rabbit and took a bite out of the stomach.

That's when the rabbit began to scream. Vince dropped the rabbit, which then proceeded to flop along the ground, leaving a smear of entrails in its wake. It was nearly eviscerated, so its movements were unnatural and looked painful. The whole pile of animals began to writhe and squirm, bringing a look of terror to Vince's face.

The rabbit screamed up at Vince again and he awoke with a start, nearly falling out of his recliner.

He barely made it to the toilet before relieving his body of the Salisbury steak, smashed potatoes and Irish whiskey.

After hugging the toilet for a long while, he crawled to his bed and closed his eyes, asleep before his cheek hit the pillow.

SEPTEMBER 14

1

Vince sat at his desk, stomach rolling, nursing a bottle of Pepto. His head pounded and he was unable to get the image of the screaming rabbit out of his head. He knew he shouldn't have drunk the whiskey the night before, but the images of the day had taken away his discretion and he had wanted to simply forget. Now it felt like a waste of good alcohol.

The muffled sounds from the bullpen penetrated his skull, causing his brain to feel like a nail was being hammered into it. He didn't know how he would get any quality detecting done, and he wished his partner were there to take the brunt of the think work.

As if the universe had heard his plea his cell phone tinkled out a notification. Lew had texted him.

> How's it going? Anything happening I should be aware of? I'm at the diner down the street if you're hungry

Despite his mood Vince smiled. Ol' reliable couldn't just sit at home and while away the couple of weeks. Being a detective was too ingrained into his being, which was not unlike how Vince felt.

He picked up his cell and tapped away letting his partner know he'd be there in twenty and to order him a rasher of eggs and sausage with some orange juice to wash it all away.

The bullpen had gone quiet, but Vince had yet to notice. He took another pull from his magic pink juice and paused with the liquid still in his mouth. It tasted like chalk mixed with strong peppermint.

When he looked up, he saw that everyone was staring at him, and the Chief was nearly jogging toward his office. He swallowed down the liquid, grimacing at the flavor, and waited for the Chief to arrive.

The Chief threw open the door and sat in a chair, trying to catch his breath. Vince waited, but not for long.

"I need you to come with me to the lobby. Now!"

Vince looked into the Chief's eyes and saw what he thought must be fear. He quickly rose and gestured for the Chief to lead the way, which he did in a hurry.

No sooner had they exited the office than Vince heard the yelling, and he quickened his pace.

2

A tall man stood in the lobby, a gun in his hand, blood dripping down his left arm. The front desk clerks were ducked below the edges of their desks. Multiple police officers were hiding around door jambs, service pistols at the ready. A recent arrestee was sitting in a plastic chair and had promptly wet himself when the man entered the precinct.

"I need to talk to Detective Aronson. It's of the utmost importance. And if I *don't* get to talk to Detective Aronson, this will not end well."

He waved the gun around again, trying to make his point. It seemed to do the job as most everyone in the room doubled down on their hiding spots.

"James, what the hell are you doing?" Vince's voice cut through the tension and the man named James relaxed a little, tears coming to his eyes.

"Man, am I glad to see you." James wiped his eyes with the back of the hand that held the gun.

"Why don't you give me the gun and let someone bandage you up and then we can talk. No need to scare all the nice people."

Vince had known James for nearly a decade. At one point he had used James as an informant, but the man had gotten into some hard drugs that ended up scrambling his brains something fierce. It only took a couple of bum leads for Vince to realize that he was of no use anymore. He tried to get James some help, but he had disappeared before Vince had a chance to even talk to him. Everyday Vince hoped he wouldn't see his name online with the words *found dead* next to it. And now he was here, bleeding out in his lobby, and looking as if someone had given him a laced drug.

Slowly, James put the gun back into his waistband, the Officers in the room tensing to jump him and drag him to the ground. One glance from Vince told them to stand down. He would handle it.

"Now, James, you know I can't have you carrying that gun while we're here at police HQ. I promise no one is going to hurt you. They just want to look at your arm and make sure you're okay. Why don't we go to my office, and someone will patch you up and you can tell me why you look like a man who has seen the depths of hell and ran away."

Vince consciously calmed his breathing and synced his respirations to James's breaths. He needed James to feel like they were on the same playing field, working together.

James grabbed his gun, the Officers jumping slightly at the movement, and then he was walking toward Vince holding it out for him to take.

After the exchange was made Vince could feel the collective relaxation from the room. He felt the weight of the gun and noticed it was off somehow. It took only a moment to realize what it was. Turning, Vince handed the gun to one of the Officers, shooting him a knowing look as the weight of the gun entered the other man's hand. The Officer felt the difference immediately and smiled.

Vince turned back to James and spun him around, cuffing him quickly and reading him his Miranda rights.

James's eyes followed the gun, and he opened his mouth to protest, but Vince shook his head slightly and James mimicked him and let the gun go…at least for the time being.

Vince looked into James's face and smiled. "Now, are you okay to walk back by yourself with Officer Woods? Or do you need a wheelchair? I'm sure we've got one around here that's not in use."

James shook his head again and replied, "Nah. I'm okay. I got

Olympian legs. They'll never give out on me."

He glanced around the room, all eyes on him, and then leaned in close to Vince, where Vince could smell the sweat and turpentine oozing out of his pores. "Can we get outta here? These people are freakin' me out, man."

Vince laughed and clapped James lightly on the shoulder. "Yeah, *they're* freaking *you* out. Let's go." He turned to one of the Officers, "Can we get medical to patch him up?"

One of the Officers nodded her head and rushed out of the room. Vince noticed the sense of relief that flooded her face as she left.

Officer Woods led James toward intake, James went to his office, and the lobby went back to business as usual.

3

James sat, admiring the bandage wrapped around his arm. Vince waited patiently. Now that James had calmed down, he had the time to wait. He had texted Lew about missing out on lunch, and so far, Lew had only texted him back fourteen times wanting to know all the details of what James was doing at the precinct. Vince ignored the texts.

The EMT stood near the door, and when Vince looked up at her, she said, "He should probably get a tetanus shot just in case. Looks like some sort of animal took a bite out of him. The pattern looks almost human—"

James interrupted the EMT. "That's because it *was* a human. Dude came right up to me and bit into my arm."

The EMT looked over at Vince, who was looking at James with sympathy. Vince thanked the EMT and asked to be left alone to talk to James. Not wanting to belabor her stay, she packed up her gear and walked out of the door.

Vince looked at James as James watched the EMT leave. He waited for James to look back at him before asking, "Did you say a human bit you?"

James nodded his head vigorously.

"James, listen to me, why would a human being want to take a bite out of you? I can smell the turpentine wafting from your pores. I'm sure you don't taste good." Vince figured he could have a bit of fun while talking to his former C.I.

"I dunno. I was just mindin' my own business and this dude came up and chomped on my arm."

Vince looked for any slip of mental capacity, but James seemed lucid. James saw the look and blurted, "I'm all here. Present and accounted for." He knocked on his head to prove his point.

"Okay, so what did this man look like?" Vince sat back in his chair, as much to get comfortable as to get away from the sickly sweet-damp smell that James seemed to be dipped in.

"I dunno. I walloped him a coupla good times in the face before he finally released me. You think he gave me some sorta sickness? You think maybe I'm gonna turn into a werewolf or somethin'?" He was starting to become agitated, and his voice was ranging higher and higher.

Vince held out his hands to try and calm him down. "I'm fairly certain you won't be turning into a werewolf any time soon, James. My guess is he was on some drugs and didn't really know what he was doing."

James nodded his head as if Vince had relayed an especially important secret to him. "I hear ya, boss. We don't need to be spreading this around, so he gets all spooked and runs off. Very smart." He tapped his head with his finger and winked.

Vince couldn't help but laugh. "James, listen. If you want to press charges, I'm sure we can get an imprint and try to match it with dental records. Is that what you want to do?"

Vince looked down at James's hands, which were moving in an intricate pattern, thumb to thumb to forefinger to thumb to middle finger and so on down the line until the pattern started over. Both hands worked effortlessly, and Vince wondered if James was even aware of what he was doing.

James remained silent for a long time, letting his fingers do their work. Finally, he looked directly at Vince and said, "Nope. I don't wanna see that dude again. I don't want to testify to nothin'. Nope. My arm feels better. I'm good. Thanks, Detective." And he stood up to leave.

"Where do you think you're going, James?" Vince asked quickly.

James thrust his thumb over his shoulder and replied, "I'm just gonna get out of here."

Vince leaned back in his seat and tilted his head to one side, amused. "You wielded a weapon, threatening police officers. Do you really think I can simply let you walk out of here?"

James's mouth worked, but not sound came out.

"I have to book you. What sort of detective would I be if I told everyone it was all okay, because I know you? Or because the gun was plastic?"

"Well, but..." James began, surprised that Vince knew the gun was plastic.

Vince stood and approached James. "Come on. It felt hollow as soon as I grabbed it. I'm sure none of the officers will want to pursue the matter any further. We have to go through the process, and you'll have an indoor space to sleep for a night."

James stood, frozen, unsure what to do next.

As Vince grabbed James by the shoulder, he thought of a question. "Where did this happen?"

James scratched his greasy scalp. Vince could hear the filth grinding under his fingernails. "I was out in the forest up in Halo, trying to find some mushr..." He stopped and stared at Vince for a long moment. "Blackberries or somethin'. I got a sweet tooth is all. And he came up and chomped."

Halo was the locals nickname for Angel's Rest. Vince wasn't surprised the forest was the scene of the crime yet again. That intuition pushed at him, informing him he was onto something. What, exactly, that something was he hadn't a clue, and he wasn't sure he really wanted to find out.

"Well, if you need anything else you know where to find me. Next time don't come into the lobby screaming and bleeding and waving a firearm."

James turned on the last point. "Speaking of that gun…" he let the unspoken question linger in the air.

"You got a permit for it?" Vince asked with a sly smile.

"Yup. It's…damn…where'd I leave that license?" James looked at Vince, a smile working its way onto his lips.

Vince shook his head. "It belongs to our lost and found now."

James rolled his eyes. "Man, now what am I gonna do if wolfman comes after me again?"

"They don't like silver. Find some and keep it on you. I'm sure it'll keep you safe."

Vince walked James to the door and motioned for an officer to come take him back to his cell and then returned to his desk and blinked a few times. The thought crossed his mind that maybe he should give up the booze, at least for the time being. He needed to be sharp and at the top of his game, especially with Lew out there twiddling his thumbs and texting him, Vince looked at his cell phone, forty-eight times at this point.

He unlocked the phone, typed out a message to Lew telling him he wanted to meet at the diner in half an hour, and as soon as he hit send, he got a message back informing Vince that he was still at the diner, so feel free to come by any time.

Vince groaned, slid the phone into his pocket, turned out the light and walked the gauntlet of looky-loos and deer-in-headlights on his way out of the building.

4

Vince walked through the front door of the diner; the bell attached at the top jangling and informing the whole place of his arrival. Lew was sitting at a booth in the far corner, a small hill of empty sugar packets sitting next to his coffee cup. Even from this distance Vince could see he was jittery, but the multitude of text messages had already prepared him for a restless partner.

Lew spotted him and waved him over, a smile parting his lips. At the same time the owner of the diner walked over to the table dropping off eggs, sausage and orange juice.

"I hope you haven't just been loitering and have been a good patron for Melinda, Lew," Vince said as he slid into the booth opposite his partner.

"Oh, he's been quite patronizing," Melinda said, a smile on her face.

Lew held his hands up. "Hey, I've been drinking coffee all day and I'm quite sure I've eaten three full meals. And here you are now with another full meal. So, that makes four."

They all laughed, and Melinda made her way to another table that was motioning for a check.

Lew leaned across the table, setting the conspiratorial mood instantly. "So, what happened?"

"Do you remember James?"

Lew nodded his head. "Yeah, that tweaker who finally snapped and disappeared. He finally find himself dead?"

The people from the tables nearby looked over at the detectives with smug disapproval on their faces. Vince was certain a few were waiting for more juicy details.

"Sorry folks. Go on about your meals. We'll talk quieter." Clear disappointment from at least three faces.

He turned back to Lew who was unabashedly eating one of Vince's sausage links.

"Sorry, I'm still hungry," he said through a mouthful of pork.

"James came into the precinct bleeding from his arm and waving a gun around."

Lew stopped chewing. "Shut up."

"It's true. It was plastic, but we didn't know at the time. And it looked like someone bit him. Or something bit him. He probably found his way into a horse pasture and an irritated nag nipped him one." Vince picked up his fork and knife and tucked into his meal.

Lew swallowed the sausage, gulped his coffee, and widened his eyes at Vince. "You don't think it was our animal muncher, do you?"

Vince shook his head and processed the question while chewing his scrambled eggs. "Just because someone mauled a bunch of animals and took big, hulking bites out of them doesn't mean that same person is going to start in on people too."

"It happened out at the forest, didn't it?"

Unsurprised by his guess, Vince nodded. "But still, there's no real connection."

"Get the bite imprints. Run them against dental records. We'll know if it's our friend in a beat."

"I couldn't convince him to do it. He's still paranoid; didn't want to press charges."

Lew leaned back and slapped his hand on the tabletop. "Damn. I still bet dollars to donuts that our good pal Martin is at the center of this."

"Don't tell me one day off work and you're already turning paranoid yourself? You've taken time off from work for a week before.

Cabin fever shouldn't have hit already."

Vince gulped his orange juice, a little spilling down his chin.

Lew absentmindedly handed Vince a napkin. "No. I just…it feels different, you know? Knowing that I can't go back in if I wanted is different than being able to cut a vacation short. This is…out of my control. All I've thought about is Martin and his Midnight munchie session. Something doesn't feel settled about it."

Vince's mouth slowly stopped chewing. He wanted to hear Lew's take on the situation and compare notes.

"I don't know if you noticed, but yesterday when we were talking to him it almost seemed like he was waiting for us to believe the things he was saying. Like he was hoping he could lie to us and get away with it."

Vince simply stared at Lew and Lew smacked himself on the forehead. "You *are* on the same page. You saw it too. He was hiding something. And now we'll never get a chance to weasel the info out of him."

After a moment, Vince shrugged. "I wouldn't be too sure."

Lew's eyes lit up. "What do you mean, buddy?"

"The feeling I got was that he knew exactly what was happening and he was planning his next move. I mean, it was much more subtle than that, but that was the sense I got."

The food he was eating lost all its flavor, the images of the disassembled animals creeping back into his mind.

"Okay, but we can't do anything until he actually commits a crime or there is an implication that he is involved in something." Lew was talking more to himself than to Vince, which was a common occurrence.

"So, what do we do? Hope he commits a crime? Pray for him to act on a nefarious scheme?" Vince liked priming Lew's thinking pump, because it always fascinated him where Lew would take the ideas.

"Maybe. I guess that's what we'll have to do. Can we get a tail on him? No. That's too much. Hunches and hunches in bunches. Can't go off a skinny thought to get a fat reward. We can research local cults. We can look up what would make a man do what he did. We can hope he does something just over the line enough for us to take him in for questioning. These are a few of my favorite ideas." Lew stopped and looked at Vince for confirmation.

"Those seem like legitimate options. At least two of them you can do from the comfort of your own bed without the Chief getting all blustery with you. And you'll have your laptop to keep you warm." Vince smiled and finished his food.

Lew rolled his eyes. "Fair enough. So, tonight I will research cults and mental problems, and you keep your ears open for any sightings of two-eyed, no horned, walking, purple people eaters. You heading back to the office?"

Vince shook his head. "I'm not feeling so great. I think I'm going to go home and rest."

Lew put on his most dramatic southern accent, "Oh, you got the vapors?" It came out sounding like *vay-puhs*. "All joking aside, I'm going to need you at your utmost if the fecal matter splatters the fan blades." He raised his voice at the last bit and smiled at the ears that pricked up hoping for one last gruesome description.

Vince offered a sad, tired smile. "I will do my best."

They settled the bill with Melinda, making sure to leave a hefty tip in their wake. The sun was beginning its descent to the other side of the world as they exited the front door, the bell at the top jingling their departure. The air smelled like autumn and the cold nipped at their faces. Vince felt like he wasn't going to be getting much sleep over the next few days.

5

Instead of going home, Vince decided to take a drive and clear his head. He was finding it difficult to focus on any one aspect of the oddity of the last two days, and that always led to a jumble of information that had to be separated, which meant more work for him.

He found himself driving the perimeter of the Angel's Rest woods, looking for something, anything that might contain the smallest hint of a clue as to what was happening.

The woods had been a protected land since long before anyone who lived in Angel's Rest had been alive. It used to belong to the Ojibwa tribe and was forcefully taken when the area was colonized. After many decades had passed, a petition was signed to declare the forest an environmentally protected land. Surveyors arrived and plotted the exact land that would constitute the extent of the protection, and a team of experts came in and decided what would be done with all the man-made additions within the bounds of the forest. Vince wasn't aware of what all was done, but he did know the forest had begun to thrive once the act had passed.

Now, as Vince stared into the forest, it felt as though hidden eyes were watching him. Something in the forest was beckoning for him to enter and learn the secrets, just as Martin had done a couple nights before. *You have gotten but a taste; come in and feast,* the trees seemed to say. Empirically, Vince knew forests didn't speak. They had no voice. But it was more than an audible tone in his head; it was a deep, soul penetration that made his mind feel fuzzy. It was a magnetic pull to discover the secrets the trees held.

He sat, staring intently at the woods for a good twenty minutes before he roused himself enough to notice movement where the grass field met the first trunks of the trees. Instinctively, he leaned forward, but the rustling was too subtle to know if it was real or his mind playing tricks on him. He turned the lights of his car to full bright and caught a glimpse of a set of eyes reflecting the light. They were gone so quickly Vince surmised they were the eyes of a fox or maybe a deer.

After a few moments, Vince realized he was holding his breath and he released it forcefully, allowing a sharp *HAW* to escape with it. On a hunch, he rolled down his window and listened to the breeze slide through the trees. The sound was mesmerizing, and he felt himself moving to the rhythm, his eyes closing.

His hand slowly moved to the door handle, and he would have opened the door if his intuition hadn't kicked in allowing him to realize there was something missing from the sounds of the forest. He heard the wind, the distant drone of the highway, the faint buzz of neon signs in town. What he didn't hear was any wildlife. There were no crickets, frogs, or nocturnal birds making noise. The chill returned, making him shudder in his seat. Something was wrong.

Before he knew what he was doing he was out of his car, his hand groping for his hip to make sure his weapon was there. His cell phone chirped, making his heart jump into his throat. Ignoring his phone, he took a few steps toward the forest. He silently made his way to the edge of the forest, the whispering wind beckoning him to enter. He felt as in a daze; almost like being hypnotized. A distant thrumming sound filled his ears and he imagined it as a heartbeat in the center of the woods, pumping life to plant and animal alike. He could see the veins of the leaves moving nutrients to sustain life, and the roots of the trees acting as arteries, returning the lifeblood back to the heart. The canopy of foliage acted as protection for its creatures, but now the animals were in danger, and the forest was in defense mode. Nothing would be allowed within unless it passed the examination. Vince felt all this and hesitated to step past the boundary. He knew that if he set one foot in the forest, he would be submitting himself to this test, and if he failed, he would be torn limb from limb by the sentient guardians that towered within. He didn't dare tempt that bit of fate. In his dozing state he looked down and watched his right foot cross the threshold, break the boundary, disobey his non-verbal commands to stay put, and he closed his eyes, waiting for a tree branch to impale him so the animals of the forest could seek their revenge and feast on his lifeless body.

But nothing happened. He breathed the air in, smelling the coppery scent of blood in the air. And he knew he was near the spot where they had found Martin, and he also knew that the smell would linger for weeks, simply because of the amount of blood that had spilled.

He felt a tear fall onto his cheek and absent-mindedly swiped it away. A new sound came to him then as the winds shifted direction. There *was* a thrumming sound, but it was more of a bass drum beat than a heart. It sounded like music was being played somewhere in the forest. A trance-like EDM beat that only added to the hypnotic feeling. Vince knew he shouldn't investigate, but he felt that if he didn't and he got a call in the morning about more strange happenings in the woods, he wouldn't be able to forgive himself.

His feet carried him ten feet into the forest before he stopped again, listening for the music. It took a moment, but there it was, a bit more distinct now. Vince continued deeper into the forest, allowing himself to be led by the steady, throbbing beat. A small animal skittered past his feet, but he hardly noticed. He was in stalking mode, his senses focused on the task at hand.

An image flashed into his head of the time he had pinned a

suspect inside an abandoned apartment complex, and the man, an acclaimed junkie who had attempted rehab multiple times, blasted music in an attempt to disorient him. But it was an amateur idea, because in academy one of the drills was focus under confusion. The confusion could include disorienting lighting, random squeaks and groans, and loud music. Instead of chasing the man to the music, he had flanked the area and gotten behind the man who thought he was safe hiding under a bedframe made of springs and metal. To the man's credit, he didn't struggle once he was found, but he was surprised to have been discovered so quickly.

There had been many suspect stalking situations, but this felt different. He felt like he wasn't the only one hunting. Something else was in the forest prowling in search of him.

Vince had the sudden feeling of being exposed. It felt the way he always did when crossing a border and was asked to step out of his vehicle. He knew he wasn't carrying anything illegal, but there was always that small doubt in the back of his mind that made him think that maybe he had done something wrong on that particular day.

He noticed that his hands were slightly shaking and quite cold, so he rubbed them together to encourage blood flow. He also realized that the wind did not penetrate this far into the forest. Turning around, he expected he would not be able to see the edge of the trees, but instead discovered he was only about thirty feet from where he started. This sent a new, unpleasant sensation zinging down his spine. Everything was wrong here. There was no outcome to this scenario that encouraged him. Dread was slowly enveloping his heart and he could feel himself breathing faster, almost to the point of hyperventilation.

Vince felt his sanity start to unravel. He had no clue why walking through the forest at night would produce such anxiety, but here it was, almost freezing him in place. Somewhere deep in his head he knew that if he stopped moving, he would die. The complete irrationality of this frustrated him, but he couldn't shake it. So, he moved deeper.

Shadows leapt at him, causing him to flinch and see things that weren't there; masks in the bushes, creatures flashing sharp fangs, children hiding in trees. The braided rope that was his mind was slowly fraying and nowhere within his willpower did he have the ability to repair it. His hands were sweating, his armpits were damp, and his breathing was short and quick.

He stumbled and fell on top of a bed of mushrooms. Spores from the fungus plumed in front of him and in his panic he inhaled deeply. The spores entered his nasal cavity and he sneezed multiple times, which helped clear his head slightly. But not before he heard the sound of someone giggling in the dark.

A twig snapped to his left and the terror returned instantly. A sensation not unlike something wriggling in his brain. Then a branch snapped to his right. He was surrounded. He groped for his gun, but he couldn't unlatch the holster; his hand was too heavy and sweaty. A running sound turned his head around and he lost his equilibrium again and tumbled to the ground. Now it sounded like a group of people were running in circles around him, stirring dust into the air and rustling the leaves. Vince had never felt so frightened in his life. He put his hands over his ears and closed his eyes tight, but it did nothing except heighten the terrifying experience. He tried to scream, but nothing came out.

Out of the darkness a hand reached toward him and squeezed his shoulder. He jumped and turned, reaching for his pistol again. No one. Another hand grabbed his shoulder and he backed up against the trunk of a tree. His breathing was shallow, and he saw spots swimming in front of his eyes. Then the chanting began. A nearly silent susurrus of voices whispering just outside of eyesight. Vince blinked and rubbed his eyes, trying to make out any figure in the dark, but there was nothing. Only sound upon sound, building to a crescendo of fear wrapping its bony talons around his heart. He felt out of control, out of his body, out of his mind. He wanted to scream until his lungs collapsed, but there was nothing.

The chanting rose and he caught his first glimpse of movement. His eyes darted back and forth, but there was nothing more. He closed his eyes, willing himself to be somewhere, anywhere else but where he was. But when he opened them again, he saw it. It looked like a person, but its body was contorted in unnatural ways. It looked like it was doing a backbend, but the head was right-side-up. And it waggled from side to side, stretching on the veiny neck that throbbed as blood, or something just as viscous, coursed through it.

It moved toward him, its arms and legs crackling like firewood. The mouth opened, showing sharp, rotted teeth. He heard a deep guttural growl coming from the human-like thing that was inching ever closer. And still, he could not scream for help. He was frozen in place, his face twisted at the horror in front of him.

The mouth of the thing opened wider and folded backward over its head, revealing more teeth and the dark tube of its throat. As the face turned in on itself, Vince heard the cracking of bones and a dark, oily substance bubbled up from the gaping hole of its neck.

Vince's bladder released then, and he began to cry. The feeling of urine soaking his legs somehow snapped him out of his terror and he stood up and ran in the opposite direction of the creature that was nearly upon him. He had lost his directional bearings, but he didn't care. All he knew is he had to put as much distance between him and the abomination in the forest as possible. He blindly ran, branches reaching for him, slicing his forearms and cheeks.

For a moment he thought he saw his car between the trees, but then he heard footsteps approaching quickly and took evasive maneuvers, twisting his ankle and falling to the ground. It felt like he may have fractured his ankle, but he had more pressing issues to worry about. He tentatively put weight down and the ankle seemed to hold him, so he limped further away from the sounds of whatever was stalking him.

He came around a large tree and there, staring him directly in the face was the human-like creature, opening its mouth wider, hoping to take Vince into itself. In a last-ditch effort, he pushed the thing with all his might and turned to run and smacked his forehead against a thick branch. His teeth clicked together painfully, and he sat heavily onto the ground, his vision swimming.

He tried to stand, but everything blurred, and he vomited, and the world faded away. The last thing he heard before blackness enveloped him was the sound of his stalker chanting in some unknown language, its tongue clicking out a rhythm.

SEPTEMBER 15

1

Vince woke up abruptly, his breathing coming in quick sips. He was in bed. He was staring at the ceiling. He was alive.

Tentatively, he raised his head, but his vision swam, and he laid back down. Somehow, he had made his way back home and was lying in his bed. The last thing he remembered was being chased through the forest. His head pounded to the beat of his heart. Every thump in his chest was a hammer fall in his skull. It felt as though he had been drinking for days and his brain was trying to comprehend how it was even possible.

A soft sniff from the corner of the room alerted Vince that he wasn't alone. Alarm bells sounded, which didn't help the pain already residing in him, and he reached for his bedside table where he kept a pocket gun. The person who had sniffed rose from their chair and Vince turned his head, willing himself not to vomit from the vertigo that caused the world to spin. That's when Vince noticed he had an I.V. in his hand.

"Easy there, pal. You've got quite the lump on your head." The voice was familiar, but Vince's gray matter was sloshing about, making it hard to focus.

Vince lay back down on the bed and took a couple deep breaths. He realized the room didn't look quite to be his bedroom. "Where am I?" he croaked. His eyes searched the room as best they could, but he didn't dare try to move his head around again.

"Well, my friend, you are in the hospital. You've got a lump the size of a walnut sticking out of your forehead, and you stopped hallucinating about twenty minutes ago." The voice sounded very amused by the situation.

"I can't move my head, or I might throw up everywhere. Stand over me so I can see you."

The person shuffled over and suddenly there was a face above him, smiling broadly, chewing a piece of gum. "I thought it was only alcohol, but shrooms? Never would've guessed." Lewis chuckled and rolled his eyes.

"Shrooms? What are you talking about?" Vince tried to remember any details about the night before, but the pain was too present.

"Brother, they found a wicked amount of psilocybin in your blood. They don't know exactly what type of mushroom it was you ingested, but it was potent and registered as synthetic. Whoever supplied you needs to be taken in for tampering with the product."

Vince furrowed his brow, trying to think through the haze. "Did someone find me in the forest?"

Lew nodded. "Said you were out of your goddamn mind. Their words. Talking some crazy shit about a person with a super wide mouth, and how it was going to eat you."

"Why are you here?"

"Emergency contact. I guess you don't really want your ex showing up. Makes sense. Chief wants to know what you were doing with mushrooms. I told him I'd help figure out the mystery if he took away my suspension, and he did that little glare thing he does. You know, the one where you have to guess if he's mad or constipated?" Lewis shook his head and laughed again.

"What's so funny?" Vince was starting to lose his patience.

"The EMT said you grabbed his shirt on the way in and whispered something to him about a dingo or something? I don't know. I don't think we have dingo's around here. I just want to know what you were doing with hallucinogens. That stuff'll mess you up good." A hint of concern found its way into Lew's voice.

"I guarantee you I have not been eating mushrooms. I don't even like the garden variety ones. It's like eating a Band-Aid." Vince grimaced at the thought.

"Then why did tox come back positive? That stuff was practically swimming in your veins." Lew stepped away from Vince's line of sight and sat heavily into a chair, the cushion making a soft *whoompf* sound.

"I don't know." A thought crossed his mind. "Can you take me out to where they found me? I want to have a look around."

"You think you can stand?" Lew sounded worried.

"Only way to know is to try. I don't remember much about last night, but maybe going back will jog some memories."

Lew stood up. "All right. I'll get the nurse to discharge you and then I'll take you out there. Hang tight."

Vince closed his eyes, trying to center himself, and heard the door open and then shut.

The night before spun around like a funhouse ride. Every time he thought he caught onto a bit of information that would stick it would whirl out of his grasp and disappear. Something about whispering maybe. Was he being chased? Was he drugged by someone? None of it made any sense. There was nothing to hold onto and it was making him antsy. He didn't like being unaware of his surroundings or what was happening. No matter how much he drank he always knew where he was when he fell asleep; it was never enough to blank him.

He tried to recreate the last few days in his head: They had found that guy Martin at the edge of the woods with innumerable small animal carcasses littering the area. He had seemed a little squirrely when they asked him questions but had tried to act like he didn't know what was happening. Then his former C.I. had come into the precinct claiming someone had bit him but didn't have a particularly good description of the person, so there was nothing to go on there. After that was the diner with Lew, and then…

Raised voices could be heard through the thick wooden hospital door, but they were muffled just enough to be unintelligible. It sounded like a male arguing with a female. The voices came closer and then the door was opened roughly, and Lew stalked over to the bed and pointed his hand at Vince. "I'm telling you; the man is fine. He could do backflips if he wanted."

A nurse followed him into the room. Vince recognized her. She frequented the diner too. Her name was Alice. There was a fire in her eyes, and she looked like she was in her mid-twenties, although she was probably pushing forty. "Detective Monroe, I don't care what you think about Detective Aronson's state of mind and physical health. He ingested enough psilocybin, psilocin, and baeocystin to make an elephant go mad. He needs rest, he needs to remember what happened, and he needs to make sure his concussion doesn't get worse."

Something clicked then for Vince. He hit his head on a branch because someone had been chasing him. His ankle, something about his ankle. "Did you check my ankle?"

As he asked the question, he rolled both his ankles and immediately felt a twinge in his left foot. "The left one."

The argument stopped immediately, and Nurse Alice lifted the blanket that covered his foot and stared at it for a moment. "It's a little bruised. You might have a small contusion. Should heal up quickly with some rest and an ice heat combo."

Lew sniffed again and another piece of the puzzle clicked for Vince. "Did you swab my nostrils?"

This question took Nurse Alice completely by surprise. It took her a moment to find a response. "No. We either take blood or do a UDS, a urine drug screen. You had already urinated down your pant legs, and you were fairly unruly, so we opted to sedate you and do a blood draw. A coroner might swab your nasal cavities, but as of right now you aren't deceased, so it wouldn't be a consideration."

Vince remembered sneezing after falling into some plants. Maybe it was mushrooms. He couldn't quite solidify the image. "*Could* you please do a nasal swab? Would it return any information if I inhaled the dust of something?"

Nurse Alice shook her head. "Not likely. Especially this long after you were exposed."

Another thought occurred to him, "If I inhaled the spores of a mushroom, would that be enough to make me hallucinate?"

Lew finally caught on to the line of reasoning and piped in, "Is psilocybin potent enough to enter the bloodstream if it's aerosolized?"

At this Nurse Alice bit her bottom lip, trying to think if it was possible. "I'm no expert, but it wouldn't surprise me to find out it's possible. Many mind-altering drugs are able to be taken in various forms: ingestion, inhalation, rectal, intravenous."

She paused, gathering her thoughts. "If you found the mushrooms you think you may have come in contact with, we might be able to determine if it's possible to inhale the spores and get high."

Vince nodded at his hand. "You mind ridding me of this I.V. so I can try and find you a sample?"

Nurse Alice moved in quick and removed the I.V., placing a cotton swab and wrapping it with Coban. "I'm going to give you the address of a researcher in town who deals almost exclusively with fungus, particularly psilocybin."

She wrote a name and address and left the room so Vince could get dressed.

Lew stayed behind but was staring out the window as Vince

found his bag of clothes, which had a thin layer of dirt on them. "Couldn't get me some new clothes to wear, huh?"

"Hmmm? Oh, yeah, sorry, I didn't know your size, or I would've bought you something."

Lew turned back to the window and Vince understood he was mulling the whole event timeline in his head.

Vince startled Lew when he clapped a hand on his shoulder, informing Lew he was ready to mosey. "Don't think too hard. You're liable to get lost in there."

Lew chuckled, grabbed his jacket, and followed Vince out the door where Nurse Alice was waiting with discharge paperwork. Vince thanked her and the two men walked toward the exit both thinking about what had happened and if it all connected in some way.

2

Lew pulled up next to Vince's car, which looked like a husk of forgotten metal in the afternoon sun. Vince stood up out of the passenger seat, groaning, his head swimming, a sluggish feeling like something was perusing his brain and with it bringing a fresh bout of vertigo. Lew tried to make his way to him quickly, but Vince waved him off brusquely.

Turning to the forest, Lew frowned. "What the hell were you doing out here, Vince? It still smells like copper, doesn't it?"

Vince nodded his head slowly, making sure the world didn't tilt on him again. "Yeah." He could have been answering either question.

"Something is bugging me about our friend Martin. Seems to me he's hiding something, and I have to know what it was."

Lew shrugged. "Makes sense to me. Shall we take a gander inside the forest, see if we can't spice up our theory a little?"

Suddenly, Vince was moving toward the forest with a fixed expression on his face. He could feel the pull again; the desire to be in amongst the trees and bushes and plants. His head cleared instantly as he set foot beneath the canopy. Instinct informed him on where to go, or maybe it was that strange yearning. Lew followed close behind.

They entered a small clearing and it looked almost as if a struggle had taken place: there were broken limbs and branches, a smear of blood across the trunk of a tree. Multiple sets of footprints impacted the land, and a shred of cloth sat nestled in the middle of a growth of mushrooms. Vince pointed to it and bent low to examine the fungus, pulling his shirt up over his nose in the process.

Lew walked around the clearing, playing the possible scenario in his head as he went. The struggle didn't last long and there was a very distinct pattern of how it went. "Someone was chased through here."

"Me. I was chased. I remember something or someone coming after me. I was terrified. I guess I probably hallucinated it all, but that feeling of horror and despair was thick."

Vince checked his jacket and saw a small tear underneath his right armpit, validating the piece of cloth had come from him.

In an instant, all sound was sucked away and disappeared from the surrounding area. A high-pitched whining noise filled the emptiness and Vince clapped his hands over his ears. When that did nothing to alleviate the sound, he dug a pinkie into his ear and wiggled it, trying to reset his eardrum.

A moment later he heard Lew exclaim, "Oh Jesus. Oh my God," and Vince was on his feet, looking around for his partner.

He found him standing at the edge of the clearing, staring off into a thicket. Vince hurried up beside him and almost vomited bile onto the ground. Just beyond the thicket was another small clearing, man-made, and hanging from the branches of trees were small tokens made up of animal bones. Flies buzzed around the emblems, creating a furious humming in the immediate area.

Vince gathered himself and stepped into the clearing to investigate further. There were nearly fifty artifacts, all hanging from different tree branches, and were in the shape of animals, probably those from which the bones had come. Vince waved his hand in front of his face dispelling a hoard of flies and saw the bones were tied together using the sinews and guts of the animals. He pushed his face within inches of one of the hanging ornaments and saw tiny gnaw marks on the bones. At first guess he would say that another critter with sharp teeth had set to work on them, but he would have to bag some to send to the lab for further analysis.

"Detective Aronson!" The tone of Lew's voice, besides the fact he hardly ever referred to him as Detective Aronson, sent a chill up Vince's spine and he turned to find Lew hurling his breakfast into a bush.

As Vince approached, Lew pointed in the direction of another bundle of bones. "I think some of these might be human."

Vince moved aside a branch that was obstructing his view and instantly came to the same conclusion. He reached for his sidearm, realized it wasn't there, and put the back of his hand in front of his mouth. "What the hell is going on?"

His next move was to his cell phone. He called the Chief, explained everything, and hung up unable to stop staring at the bones the entire time.

Lew had recovered and was taking a closer look and making observations, most likely to keep himself from vomiting again. "These look like finger bones, maybe something from the leg, part of a skull. And they all have teeth marks on them. No doubt the coyotes got to them before we did."

"Do you see what was used to bind the bones?" Vince intoned.

"I see mostly intestine, maybe some hair, and tendons. We need to bag the hair to try and get an I.D. Keep a close eye on missing persons reports." Lew exhaled sharply, a soft whistle escaping his lips.

Vince continued to search the bones looking for any other clues, but he couldn't find anything more. The air pressure was heavy, pressing in on his head, making it hard to concentrate. But he fought through it, trying to remember more about the night before.

Lew clapped him on the shoulder, startling him out of his reverie. "At least now you know something was going on out here last night. I think you stumbled upon some little ritual, and you're lucky you escaped with your life. You could have ended up like our little friend over there."

Vince nodded, suddenly feeling very sleepy. There was a pulsing energy in the forest that he had never experienced before. He hadn't regularly visited the woods, but he had been there on occasion. And it had never felt as it did now. "I think our idea of a cult is looking better and better. Something we haven't encountered before."

"About time we got something fresh," Lew added with a bitter chuckle. "How long until the field team gets here?"

Vince checked his phone. "Chief said they should be here within half an hour. I didn't tell him you were with me, so if you want to get going before someone tattles…" he let the end of the sentence hang unspoken in the air.

"Nuh uh. No way I'm leaving you out here by your lonesome." Lew shook his head vigorously. "Besides, I was simply driving you back to your car from the hospital and we happened to stumble across this little scene."

"Fair enough." Vince had a thought. "Besides, I think I left my car lights on when I walked into the forest last night. It's probably dead. I might need a jump."

Lew had developed the faraway look he employed when he was responding to a conversation, but his mind was working out a problem. "See? I'm staying."

Instead of interrupting Lew further, Vince walked back out to his car to wait for the field team. He also wanted a little time to think about the whole situation. Usually the tri-cities experienced nothing more than an accidental death or drunk driver, but over the last three days they had found a guy munching on animals, he had ended up in the hospital from hallucinations, and now they had found some ritualistic holy ground in the forest. The thought crossed his mind that maybe it was time to retire.

Lew stumbled out of the forest and leaned against the hood of his car. "Okay, so here is what I'm thinking. We're dealing with some sort of cult that is heavy on the animal sacrifice. However, whatever they are hoping to accomplish isn't being brought about by woodland creatures alone, so they have escalated to humans. Maybe whatever entity they are trying to appease or invoke needs them to be more faithful, maybe they think the being is testing them."

"Retiring is starting to sound real enticing right about now," Vince responded, laying on the hood of his car.

They both sat silently for a long minute, and then they heard the crunching sound of gravel under tires and saw the field team making their approach. Vince grunted and sat up, the world tilting with him and waved at the van's driver.

When the van was parked three people exited the rear doors with kits in hand. They were dressed to the nines in protective gear and looked at Vince to guide them to the grisly scene. All of them consummate professionals with hardly a sense of humor among them. Once Lew had attempted to engage them in some light banter, and they stared at him like he had walked in naked during a family reunion. Since that incident neither Lew nor Vince were anything but strictly business.

Vince led them to the clearing where the animals were hanging and watched as they nodded to each other and pointed to different areas. They started to enter their zones, but Vince stopped them with a throat clear. "Excuse me, I need one of you to bag some mushrooms and send them to a specialist."

They all looked at each other, annoyed at being disturbed, but one of them stepped in front of Vince, giving him an impatient look. He took the young man who could have been no more than twenty, over to the grouping of mushrooms. "I need a clump of this bagged and sent to this gentleman here."

He fished out the piece of paper with the name and address. "Please include one of my cards and write a note to let him know I would like to speak with him at his earliest convenience."

The tech glared at him, but Vince wasn't fazed.

"Why don't you take a bag, put some of the mushrooms in the bag, and take them to this guy yourself?"

Vince took a step forward to test the young man's mettle, and when he didn't so much as blink, Vince knew he had no authority here in his eyes. "Listen, I need you to do me this favor. You're wearing the PPE. I'm not."

He turned away from the tech who now wore a deep scowl on his face and finished, "And besides, it's your job to lose. I can have a little chat with the Chief."

He knew the line would have little to no effect on the kid, but he couldn't help himself. As he walked toward the edge of the forest Vince saw Lew trying to hold in a smile, unsuccessfully. "He flip me off?"

Lew laughed. "Both hands. A little hip action in there for good measure. Did I tell you he's my brother's brother-in-law's stepson? Brilliant kid, but dry as a month-old bread crust."

At that they both laughed and made sure to look back at the tech who was still staring after them. The tech stared defiantly back, which made them laugh harder, and he finally turned to do his job.

"I should probably go have a sit down with the Chief to make sure I don't get fired for shroom use. Give a guy a jump?"

Lew smiled brilliantly. "Sure thing, pal. It's not like I have anything better to do."

3

Vince walked into the police station as the sun disappeared over the horizon, casting an eerie bloody glow across the landscape. He knew immediately that word had gotten around about his *episode* the night before. Avoiding their glances, he beelined it for the Chief's office, whom he found sitting behind his desk clicking a pen incessantly.

He glanced up when Vince walked in, but then went back to staring at his computer screen. "Explain."

"I followed a hunch last night. I went back out to the woods and stumbled across something I wasn't meant to stumble across. Fell into a patch of mushrooms and inhaled psilocybin. Found myself in the hospital this morning. Went back out to get my car and found some sort of altar where a ritual was performed." Vince took a seat in the only other chair in the room and waited.

The Chief had a way of letting silences spin on and on until they were so uncomfortable even a mime would break. But Vince was used to it, so he sat and waited. Finally, the Chief looked up at him and said, "Fine. Does it look like cult activity?"

"Based on what we found that is the only determination at this point."

"We?"

Vince looked away for a split second and then answered. "Lew picked me up from the hospital and drove me back to my car. We decided to take a little walk."

Silence. Then, "Fine. Just as long as he doesn't show up on the report."

"No, sir. But I could really use him right now."

The Chief sighed, looking exasperated. "No. If I renege on the suspension, I will have IA up my ass about why I'm playing favorites. I need you to listen real close, Detective Aronson."

Vince leaned in a little and the Chief's eyes locked onto his. "I don't want to see or hear about Detective Monroe having anything to do with this case until he is off his suspension. He is not to come near the precinct, and he is not to randomly appear at any more crime scenes. Am I clear?"

Vince nodded his head and sat back in the chair. "Crystal. Do you have anyone else I could team up with to do some of the leg work?"

The Chief looked almost disappointed. "Nope. No one else is able to do what Detective Monroe can."

"But you don't want him—"

The Chief interrupted him. "I don't want to hear or see him until his suspension is up." And he physically swiveled his seat away from Vince.

It took another moment for Vince to realize exactly what the Chief was telling him, but once it clicked, he immediately stood, trying to make a scene, and yelled, "Fine! I'll do it on my own!"

He turned on his heel and briskly walked through the Chief's door with an angry expression on his face. The looky-loos continued to stare, and Vince was glad for it. Misinterpreted motives made for helpful rumors.

4

Vince paced his small shed that was backed up against the woods behind his house. Absent-mindedly he began cleaning and tidying while his brain came up with a plan. If Lew were not allowed at the precinct or at any of the crime scenes, he would essentially have to fill him in somewhere else, where there were no prying eyes or lustful ears trying to catch the juicy gossip. In other words, he needed a place to problem solve with Lew where there would be no witnesses.

He continued to bustle around his shed, unconsciously whistling tunelessly through his parched lips. On the bright side, he would be able to hone his memory and verbal skills when it came to relaying information to Lew. And the concept of one sense heightening when another is removed could prove especially useful for attacking the problem from different angles. Questions might occur to Lew that Vince hadn't even thought of in the moment.

Having come up with a pseudo-plan on how to approach the limitations of working with his partner, Vince looked around his shed and realized he had tidied it up quite nicely. It finally clicked that this was the place where he would debrief Lew on all that was happening with the case. They could meet in the shed every evening and no one would be the wiser. As long as Lew could keep this to himself and not run his mouth.

He picked up his cell phone and told Lew the plan. It only took a few minutes to receive a text back and there were far too many exclamation points for Vince's liking, but the agreement was in place. Every evening they would meet in the shed to discuss the day's happenings and try and figure out where to go from there.

The only problem was there was no internet connection that far from the house, so Vince made a note to himself to contact the internet company and figure a workaround.

Satisfied, Vince located a couple fold out chairs in the corner and put them at the unfinished table in the center of the room. Then he grabbed his phone and made some notes of things he would need: Whiteboard, Markers, Drink Fridge, Pads of Paper, Pens.

He stood back and admired the space, shut the light off, and walked back toward the house.

The wind rustled through the trees, imitating the soft whispers of a pair of lovers sharing secrets. Vince knew the walkway perfectly and closed his eyes for a few seconds while he walked, allowing the night to soak into him. The air was fresh and cool on his face and for a moment he was able to disappear from the wild storm of the last few days. As he opened his eyes, he felt a small rush of wind against his left ear and heard a voice whisper: *We have a place for you, Detective.* Vince scanned his surroundings but there was no indication that anyone was nearby. He cursed his head for projecting and hurried his step a bit to quickly reach the house.

Once inside, Vince looked out of the picture windows in his living room, hoping to see something in the forest that would confirm that someone had whispered in his ear, but the more he looked the less he saw, and his last thought before turning away for the night was, *can't see the forest for the trees.*

SEPTEMBER 16

1

The sun rose over the horizon highlighting the dew on the grass. Everything was peaceful and new, hardly a vehicle on the road, the city rising from its slumber. Nothing about the morning indicated any knowledge of the preceding events.

A solitary man laced up his running shoes and set his watch to record his morning jog. After a minute or two of stretching the man hit another button on his watch, sending music blaring through his earbuds, silencing the rest of the world around him.

His run would take him partway around the perimeter of the Angel's Rest Forest and then plunge him deep into the heart of the woods, dodging along the labyrinthine paths that crisscrossed through the whole area.

After a few cleansing breaths, he took off at a brief pace, feeling the cool of the morning dissipate as his thermodynamic temperature took over to compensate for the difference between air and skin. He lost himself in the rhythm of his feet hitting the dirt path that skirted the forest, and then he saw the opening he was looking for and changed direction abruptly, heading into the depths between shrubs and ferns, oak and pine trees towering above him.

He had run this forest so many times he could close his eyes and wind his way perfectly from one side to the other: a left, a right, straight, left, left, winding path that led to the halfway point.

As he approached the halfway mark of the forest, he noticed a splash of red on some of the ferns near the trail. He figured an animal had been injured and was probably dead by now. A few paces further and he saw a large splotch of crimson and this time he slowed down a bit.

Rounding a corner, he saw a pool of blood and that made him come to a complete stop, a puff of dust rising up and surrounding his head. He took out one of his earbuds and listened to the sound of his own rapid breathing. Maybe the animal was still alive and needed help. So, he took a deep breath and held it, the sound of his heart pounding in his ears. But as his heartbeat slowed, he became aware of a whimpering sound. Something was near and it was very injured.

He took a step toward where he thought the sound was, but it grew fainter. The familiar woods suddenly took on a disorienting feeling, and a wave of vertigo rushed through the man's body. He held out a hand to steady himself and felt something slick between his hand and the tree trunk he had leaned against. Quickly he took his hand away, noticing the blood, and willed himself not to vomit.

The whimper came once again, breaking him out of his disgust. This time when he took a few steps the sound became louder. He noticed another swatch of blood on the ground by a bend in the path. Slowly, he made his way around the corner and when he looked up his face went white, and he finally did throw up his breakfast. He looked back up to confirm what he thought he had seen, and when there was no doubt in his mind, he fumbled around for his cell phone and willed his fingers to dial 9-1-1.

2

Vincent Aronson woke up naturally, no hangover headache, no calls on his cell phone, simply the sound of birds having their morning conversations outside his window.

It was the first time Vince could remember in a long time where he didn't wake up feeling worse than the day before. He assumed he must have been so busy coming up with a plan to continue working with Lew that he had simply forgotten to drink himself dark. Not that waking up feeling somewhat refreshed wasn't a nice change, but it was certainly a bit disorienting.

His natural awakening didn't last long as he heard the vibration of his phone rattle his bedside table. After stretching, feeling the cracks of his joints as he did, he reached over and saw it was the head of the crime scene department. He answered. "Talk to me."

"Vince." The familiarity did nothing except arouse tension in Vince's body. "Shit."

Something was horribly wrong. And if the head of the crime scene division was this rattled…

Dread settled in the pit of Vince's stomach. "Officer Gray. Grace. Take a deep breath and tell me what is going on."

Silence for a long moment, and then, "You need to get out here. Now." And the phone went dead.

Vince didn't need her to tell him where 'here' was, he knew. The pit in his stomach grew, and his head felt fuzzy. Something told him what he was walking into was a little worse than a few animals being eaten raw. After a few moments Vince lifted himself off the bed, got dressed, and left for the forest.

3

The grass crunched under Vince's feet in an unsatisfying way, putting him more on edge than he already was. It appeared to him that the entire police force had turned up for this event, and there was even a group of gawkers and looky-loos that had been barricaded from entering the scene.

He saw Officer Gray talking to one of her assistants and headed her direction. She was jabbing her finger at a piece of paper and didn't notice Vince until he was five feet from her.

Gray stared at Vince for a long moment, trying to figure out the best way to say what needed to be said. Finally, she settled on, "Come with me," and turned on her heel, heading into the forest.

As they walked the paths Vince noticed someone had chalked trees indicating which way they needed to go to get to the scene.

Gray spoke in clipped sentences. "He's still alive. We have paramedics here. They're giving him I.V. fluids. It doesn't look good."

Vince knew better than to ask any questions; the woman was barely holding it together as it was.

They came to a sharp curve in the path and Gray abruptly stopped, causing Vince to almost run into her.

She turned to him, and he saw the fire in her eyes. "What you are about to see..." she took a deep breath, "Vince, you've never seen anything like what you're about to see. Do me a favor and don't ask stupid questions. The paramedics are doing all they can for the man and have assured me if they move him, he will die instantly. He is going to die, but we need him alive for a bit longer. It may seem cruel, but if this is just the beginning, we need as much information as we can get to prevent it from happening again. Nod your head if you understand."

Vince pushed past her and rounded the corner. What he saw made him take a step back and he tripped over a small root, landing hard on his butt. Gray had been right; he had never seen anything like this before. He doubted anyone in the state had seen anything like it. His lips curled away from his teeth in a sneer of disgust.

Ten feet in front of him, pinned to a large tree was a man, if he could be referred to as such at this point, flayed open from neck to crotch. The folds of skin were tacked to the trunk of the tree, fully exposing the inner working of this human. There were burn marks near vital organs and along the skin line that looked as though someone had taken a blowtorch to the man, no doubt an attempt at crude cautery. An I.V. had been set up, hanging from a tree branch, feeding the man vital fluids to keep him alive.

The man was naked, and his head was slowly lolling from one side to the other. He was barely conscious, a soft moaning escaping his lips. Vince saw that his heart was beating very slowly and as he scanned the man's torso, he saw that his spleen was missing, and there were a couple incisions near the liver, but they looked interrupted. This man was going to die very soon.

Then he saw his face and reality tried to leap away from him. The man on the tree was James, his old C.I. This is the man who had two days prior come into the precinct to tell him about someone biting him. And now he was hanging from a tree, clinging to life.

A rage kindled inside Vince, and he stood up quickly, approaching the paramedics. He reached out and whirled one of them around. "Who told you to torture this man?" he demanded.

The paramedic opened and shut his mouth a few times, and then turned his eyes to someone else. Vince turned to look and saw who must have been the senior paramedic. He turned on his heel and stalked up to the other man, asking the same question.

The senior paramedic held up his hands to calm Vince, and replied, "The Chief wants to know if the man knows anything."

"You're joking, right? The chief is out of his mind if he thinks this man will ever speak again." Vince felt the rage boiling inside.

"Look, Aronson, I'm doing my job, and my job is to keep this man alive as long as we can."

The paramedic tried to turn away, but Vince spun him back around. "His name is James, and you know damn well he has hours, maybe only minutes, to live. Even if he miraculously opened his mouth and words came out, none of it would be coherent. He is septic. He is dying. Let him die."

The paramedic looked off into the distance, squinted his eyes, and then looked back at Vince. "I'm just doing my job. We have one more bag of fluids in our emergency supply and once that's gone there is nothing we can do for him. So, stick around a few minutes and maybe you will be able to get something useful from him before he's gone."

Vince's blood was boiling, and in that moment, he knew he hated the paramedic and would do everything in his power to remove him from his position.

"I refuse to be party to this bullsh—" He was cut off by a high-pitched wailing sound coming from James's direction.

Everyone turned their attention to the sound and saw James had opened his eyes wide and was screaming. The pain within the vocalization made Vince reach for his belt where his service pistol hung. As his hand gripped the butt of the gun, he took a few steps toward the man, fully intending to end the madness right then and there. But James let out one last primal scream, wrenched the arm that held the I.V. away from the tree, ripping the needle out of his arm in the process, and hunched forward, blood miraculously trickling out his mouth.

Vince, and everyone else, watched as the James's heart beat slower and slower and then stopped. The silence at the scene was profound. They could feel the essence of another person leaving the clearing. No one dared interrupt the sacred silence.

Finally, Vince could take it no longer and he glared at everyone individually before speaking in a soft, intense voice. "Every single one of you who agreed to torture this man will be lucky to have a job come tomorrow morning. I don't give a shit if you were following orders. You allowed a man to hang from a tree, clinging to life, in agony, in hopes that he would, what? Point us in the right direction on who did this to him? Provide us with some clues to follow up? Every one of you has enough training to know that man wasn't going to live. His spleen is gone, and someone ruptured his liver with a cutting tool."

As Vince spoke, he saw that most of the people present were avoiding eye contact with him. They knew what they had done, and now they had to live with it.

"We are here to serve and protect. You did not serve this man by keeping him alive. You did not protect him by allowing him to die. You tortured him." Vince's breathing was rapid, and he could feel the spit exiting his mouth as he seethed.

He turned to leave but whirled back to inject one last piece of anger into the atmosphere. "Sometimes it's okay to defy an order. Sometimes it's the human thing to do; the decent thing to do. And each and every one of you," he pointed an accusatory finger around the silent clearing, "that had a part in this atrocity will have to atone for your lack of judgment. Because what happened here today was royally fucked!"

Then he really did rush off the scene, knowing he had one more person to lay into before the day was out.

No one dared move or speak or breathe until they were positive Vince had completely evacuated the area. And even then, everyone spoke in hushed tones. They knew full well what had happened, and they also knew that what Detective Aronson had accused them of, was justified.

4

Vince pushed through the Chief's door, allowing it to bang loudly against the wall. The truth was most of Vince's anger had ebbed away on his drive over, but he still needed to make his point. He heard the Chief crunch down on his lit cigar, a bitter look crossing his face.

"How could you authorize what you did? You talk about suspending Lew, and then you toy with a man's life. Why?"

He felt disjointed in his questioning, but he had to get it out before the Chief could try and calm him anymore.

The Chief held up a hand, looked at the chewed cigar, and threw it in the trash, picking pieces of tobacco off his tongue before responding. "The extent of the man's injuries was highly under-represented. The paramedic told me he looked like he could pull through, so I gave them the authority to do what they needed to try and get information."

Vince opened his mouth, but the Chief continued, "I received report from Officer Jansen that the man was far from recovering just a few minutes ago. I should have gotten more details before making my decision."

Vince paced the room, trying with great difficulty to keep his seething self-righteous anger afloat, but it was steadily sinking. The Chief watched him pace with his eyes, waiting for the right moment.

"What did you see when you were there?" the Chief asked quietly after about a minute of tense silence.

"It was James. James was filleted like a fish. His skin was tacked to the trunk of the tree where he was hung; two large spikes through his shoulders, placed properly to hold the weight for a long time without tearing through the flesh. His spleen was gone. His liver had lacerations and a slight tear. Most likely he was septic. I wouldn't be surprised if a few liters of blood had been lost."

Vince took a deep breath, taking himself back to the scene in his mind. The Chief waited, grabbing a new cigar out of his desk.

"The wounds were cauterized, enough to keep him alive until," he waved his hand, indicating the sick display he had seen leading to the man's death, "and I wouldn't be surprised if the tool used was a blowtorch, but it looked like someone had at least looked up organ removal and cautery online to prolong the suffering." Vince stopped and looked at the Chief.

The Chief nodded at him, rolled the cigar between his lips and asked, "Anything else?"

Vince took a deep breath, forcing himself into Detective mode once more. His eyes moved back and forth like a metronome as he added three dimensions to his memory, allowing himself to move freely in the scene.

"I think his kidneys were removed. There was a blood smear on either side of his body on the trunk that wasn't consistent with the blood spatter of anything caused by what was done to the front side of him."

The Chief leaned back in his chair, causing the back of it to groan in protest. The sound knocked Vince out of his head, but not before he saw one last thing that he hadn't mentioned at the actual scene. He looked directly at the Chief and said, "They cut his tongue out. Why cut out his tongue? The extent of the damage done to his body was enough to kill him. Why..." his voice trailed off as he tried to think of any rational idea, but nothing came to him.

"Where do you go from here?" the Chief asked quietly.

"I only have one possible lead, but it's a stretchy one. I have to leap a few chasms to get to my destination." Vince was talking more to himself than the Chief, but the Chief kept prodding.

"Gut level?"

"The gut is strong."

"Enough to make me proud?"

Vince nodded.

"I don't want to hear anything about it until you have absolute proof to show for it."

"Copy." Vince was away from the conversation now, but he would remember each detail in the lockbox of his mind that kept case details in pristine condition until he needed them.

The Chief said nothing more and Vince slowly made his way out of the office, making mental notes about next steps. The officers he passed saw the look on his face and knew better than to break through the hypnosis, lest they cause him to forget a vital piece of information.

As he exited the precinct, he knew his next step was his first meeting with Lew in the shed behind his house. The prep for the room would have to wait for another day. Time was precious now that a human had been sacrificed. What he did next was crucial to stop it from happening again. He was home before he fully realized he had left the Chief's office, but he had more important things to worry about.

5

Lew leaned against a wall, watching Vince intently. Vince had already given him all of the details of the day and they were both trying to figure out how to proceed without it coming back to bite them in the ass.

"If we bring him back here, he can immediately lawyer up and anything we have done looks beautifully suspicious." Lew shrugged his shoulders.

"What if I talk to him down at the precinct? Let him know something similar happened near where he was found and hopefully his memory has returned enough that he can be of some help?"

The idea sounded thin, even to himself, but Vince knew they were both grasping at sand.

"We know where he works. You get his contact info and ask him to come on down for a chit chat, a follow-up on the unpleasantness of a few days ago. Read him as best you can and relay it all to me. Do you think he would be okay with you recording it? Sure would make it a lot easier." Vince could sense the frustration coming from his partner, but the idea wasn't half bad.

"Okay, I will get him there. Maybe I can be bold enough to get you in on a video call with him." Vince chewed the inside of his cheek. "Everything about this is rotten. I don't like it one bit."

"We've never had anything similar to this. CSI didn't find any evidence to run with, and we've only seen Martin showing up at the edge of the woods to link any of this. I feel like we're running out on a frozen lake without checking for thickness. One wrong move and we're plunging into the icy waters of shit creek." Lew slammed his open palm against the wall.

Vince sat down on his heels, running the scenarios in his head of what could possibly go wrong, and he wasn't satisfied with any outcome. Finally, he sighed and looked directly at Lew.

"You okay with us losing our jobs?"

Lew pushed himself off the wall and stared back at Vince. "Why are we there now?"

"We have nothing to go on. Our guts agree that Martin has a part in all this. But that is a fart in the wind as far as evidence is concerned. This stops being a legitimate police investigation and becomes a rogue operation. I can take it as far as possible within the walls of the precinct, but if Martin starts to smell something rotten, we whisk him away to a vacation in the shed. If we are wrong about any of it," he paused, taking a deep breath. "Even if we're right about all of it, we will most likely lose our jobs. So, is it worth it to you to lose your job if it means putting a stop to whatever cluster has popped up in our neck of the woods?"

Lew frowned and shrugged his shoulders. "I've got nothing better to do. Let's give it a go. Who knows? The tri-cities are small enough, maybe we get a slap and suspension. Hell, I'm already suspended, so I'll just extend my leave."

Vince stared at him for a long moment and then nodded his head, resolute. "Then it's settled. Tomorrow I'll get Martin to the station, dial you in, have a conversation with him, and play the entire case on instinct."

Lew mockingly shivered. "Exhilarating."

With that step taken, they both felt an ominous weight come over them. The seeds of doubt wound their way into the soil of their minds, but neither expressed the flash of fear. They knew if they voiced any more concerns, it would throw them off the trail and even their intuition would betray them. And that would leave them with absolutely nothing.

So, they nodded to each other and without another word Lew walked out the door and Vince made his way back to the house. The world was about to shift, and they needed to be as prepared as possible.

SEPTEMBER 17

1

Convincing Martin to come down to the station proved surprisingly easy. He told Vince that he had the day off with zero plans, and he'd always wanted to sit in an interrogation room. When Vince had mentioned they could simply talk in his office Martin had insisted they do it like on the TV, as long as Vince promised not to rough him up. And no handcuffs because he was claustrophobic.

So, they sat in the interrogation room, Martin munching on some beef jerky and sipping a coffee, Vince sitting on the other side of the table trying to get in touch with Lew. After getting his voicemail for the third time he gave up and asked Martin if he could simply record the conversation instead. Martin happily agreed, crumbs from the crackers spilling over his lips.

"All right, Martin. I just wanted to ask you a few questions about the other day. Specifically, if you remember anything more about what happened." Vince waited for him to wash a mouthful of jerky down with a swig of coffee.

Martin grimaced and tossed the packet of crackers onto the table. "You got anything with some flavor? These crackers taste like dust."

Vince shrugged his shoulders and remained silent.

Martin stared at him for a long moment and then said, "Man, I'm telling you it's like a big blank space. One minute I'm walking through the woods and the next I'm horking down Thumper and friends." He shrugged his shoulders.

"So, you remember eating them then?"

"What? Oh, no. I guess I remember after that. With you guys showing up and me feeling sick and stuff."

Vince noticed that Martin's demeanor was a lot more relaxed and go with the flow then their initial encounter, which made sense. Martin took a handful of jerky and shoved it into his mouth, bits dribbling out and falling to the table. Martin unceremoniously wiped those away and set about chewing loudly. He seemed to be going through the motions of eating rather than enjoying it.

"So, nothing at all. No dreams or sudden memories? Nothing strange popping into your head?"

Martin slowed his chewing, his eyes moving back and forth, his tongue sucking at a lodged piece of jerky. The sounds were putting Vince on edge, but he fought the urge to yell at his guest.

Finally, Martin shook his head and replied, "Nah. Nothing at all. It's like someone reached inside and snipped that night right out of there." He smiled, jerky sticking out between his teeth.

Vince sat back in his chair heavily. He didn't know where to go with the questioning. There was nothing he could think of that would put him on the right path. It felt like he was stalled in the center lane of a busy highway.

"Well, Martin, I feel like I've wasted your time. I apologize. Have yourself a good day. Thank you for coming down here." He stood up and offered his hand.

Martin jumped out of his seat, a cascade of jerky bits falling from his shirt. "Not a problem. It was fun being interrogated. Hopefully, I don't have to do this for real anytime soon."

He took Vince's hand and as they shook Vince had one last Hail Mary pass through his head. "When you were walking in the woods did you run across any strange mushrooms?"

The air in the room immediately changed and Martin's hand squeezed down on Vince's. His jaw muscles worked, tensing and releasing in rhythm. This was it. Vince had finally hit on something important. Everything that had happened that night was released with this question. Vince didn't believe that he had unlocked hidden information; it felt more like the question gave him permission to know more. But Martin still held out in a last-ditch effort.

"Mushrooms?" There was a wild look in Martin's eyes. Vince could feel the young man's hand trying to loosen its grip, but he wasn't succeeding. So, Vince increased the pressure of his grip and Martin's eyes widened.

"The mushrooms, Martin."

They remained at stalemate for a long moment, Martin's breathing quickening, a bead of sweat popping out on his forehead. And then he broke it with a single question, "What did you see, Detective?"

Vince forcibly removed his hand from Martin's grip, but Martin didn't move. He stared intently at Vince, waiting for an answer. "What makes you think I saw something?"

"You wouldn't ask about the mushrooms unless something happened." Vince felt the shift in tone immediately. There was now a mixture of menace and awe in the man's voice, and it chilled him to the bone. "So, tell me what you saw."

"Something unreal. Something not there. A human-like being."

"Rows of teeth?"

Vince blinked involuntarily. Martin looked ravenous for the information.

"Yes. The mouth folded back on itself. Like I said, a hallucination."

Martin finally moved, seating himself back at the table, never taking his eyes off Vince. "Oh, no no no. Not a hallucination, Detective. It was all very real. As real as you and me." With that he reached across the table and pushed Vince softly in the shoulder.

"I ended up in the hospital, Martin. Do you know what psilocybin is?" Vince felt a sense of dread wash over him, but he knew without a doubt that he had simply hallucinated. Could mushrooms create a mutual event?

A smile slowly grew on Martin's face, as if he knew where the key was to a lock that would open up a whole new world. Vince thought the smile said that he now had someone to share the experience. He had someone who would believe him. Martin stared at Vince, watching every movement with his eyes alight.

"Martin, I need you to listen to me. I woke up in the hospital and they told me I had psilocybin in my system. Whatever I saw the night before I hallucinated. I fell and knocked myself unconscious and someone called an ambulance and got me to the hospital."

Vince knew that repeating words and names was a calming technique. It could also help someone who was nearing a psychotic break, as Martin appeared to be in this moment.

Martin shook his head slowly. "No, Detective. No. You want it to be a hallucination, so you make it so. You had your brain melted and you couldn't handle it. It tested your sanity and left you wanting."

Suddenly, Martin reached across the desk and grabbed both of Vince's hands in his. "Did you meet him?"

"Meet who, Martin?" Vince tried to pull his hands away, but Martin's grip was like a vise.

"Him. The one whom all this is for. The Master." Frustration edged into Martin's voice. A chill inched its way down Vince's spine.

"I didn't meet anyone in the forest. I hallucinated—"

"Bullshit! It was not. It. Was. Not! A hallucination. Stop saying that. It is disrespectful." Vince was stunned into silence by the interruption.

Martin's eyes shifted to the side. "Maybe you aren't ready yet. Maybe you need more time. You got a taste to see if you were worthy." His eyes flicked back to Vince. "And you're here. That must be significant. But why wait?"

Martin's eyes flicked back and forth as if he were trying to work out a puzzle in his head.

Vince opened his mouth to say something, but Martin's eyes focused, and he retightened his grip on Vince's hands. "I know. I get it. Of course. You are analytical. It has to be proved to you. That must be the reason."

Vince noted a slide into a tone of hysteria and knew he needed to stop it, or he could be in danger. "Martin! Who are you talking about? Who is the master?"

A sinister smile spread across Martin's face, and he released a low cackle before replying, "The Wendigo, of course. He will show himself to you when you are ready. His bonds have been broken and he is growing stronger. He has been held captive for so long that he must regain his strength. And we give him the strength. We bring it to him. And he feasts. And the connection among all his disciples grows stronger. You will be one of us. You will be among us. Soon. I know it."

Vince stared across the table at this now giddy man who had fed his own delusions long enough to believe what he was saying. It amazed him how quickly someone could fall under the spell of their own delusions. And then it struck Vince what Martin had given away during his diatribe.

"You said 'we', Martin. How many of us are there?"

Martin looked up hopefully. "So, you believe?"

"Give me time," he replied, hoping to get his answer. "How many?"

Martin looked down, his mouth silently moving as he thought about the question. "I know of seven. The pilgrimage has begun.

There will be more. Hundreds by the Equinox. So says the Wendigo."

Vince truly hoped the disbelief didn't show on his face, and he was afraid if he kept pushing the questions Martin would see through his ruse. But he needed more information. "Can I meet the others?"

Martin broke out of his semi-trance and frowned at Vince. "Not until you are ready. Of course not. Once you have been marked, then you will know each of us. And we will know you." He nodded his head, coming to some conclusion. "That's why I felt a slight vibration. You are on your way to enlightenment. But you aren't there yet. That's why it's faint. I see that now. I understand that now."

Vince tried to remember everything Martin had said, but there was so much information. He would have to run the recording back to formulate his next move. He glanced over at his phone. A line of zeroes showed on the screen. He had forgotten to start recording.

Martin released Vince's hands and Vince pulled them away, feeling the ache in his joints. There was a satisfied grin on Martin's face and Vince was unsure if he could safely let him leave the precinct. He might hurt someone. But he had nothing to go on outside of the lunatic ramblings of the last twenty minutes. He couldn't legally detain him unless he threatened to harm another person, and even then, it was sketchy.

He took a deep breath and tried to rub the pain out of his hands. "Martin, I need to ask you one last question, and then I will see you out." Martin nodded his head eagerly.

"When you said you had to feed the master to give him his strength, what did you mean?" Vince inhaled sharply after asking the question, unsure if the man sitting in front of him would give him the answer he needed or finally figure out that Vince wasn't on board with all this Wendigo, mythological creature fantasy and shut it all down.

"Detective, you found me the morning after I had regained *my* strength, so surely you already know the answer."

He stood up and bowed slightly. "I will meditate and await your entrance into the Master's fold."

And with that Martin walked toward the door. He paused with his hand on the knob and turned one last time to speak to Vince. "These are exciting times, and we will all be glad we are on the side of the Wendigo when it is all over. Until next time, Detective."

Martin walked out the door and Vince slumped down in his seat, trying to catch his breath. Whatever was happening was far worse than he had originally thought. He understood now that the man in the woods was a sacrifice to this Wendigo myth and knew that there would be more if they were unable to stop this new cult. But, in order to stop them, Vince needed to put a tail on Martin, and he knew just the suspended Detective for the job.

He nearly had his heart rate under control when his phone buzzed loudly on the steel tabletop. After a moment he looked over and saw the caller I.D. It was Lew. He hit the answer button.

2

Vince sat at his desk for a long while, staring at the door opposite him. He was trying to wrap his head around the interview he had just conducted with Martin. The conclusions he had come to so far were that the mushrooms were at the center of this cult, and he needed to figure out how to stop it before they sacrificed another person to their *master*.

He was frustrated with Lew until he found out that Lew had in fact gotten stuck following a lead on the cult. After their discussion the night prior, he had decided to stake out the forest and had run across a group of young adults congregating near the location of the murder. Instead of frightening them and risking someone at the precinct hearing about his snooping, he had watched them. They stayed there all night, not eating, not drinking, simply sitting and staring into the woods.

As the sun crested the horizon they had simply stood up and walked off, Lew commenting on them looking a bit disappointed. The best he could tell, they were cult wannabes hoping for an invitation.

After that he had gone home and promptly passed out and awakened only minutes before calling Vince. Lew's instincts screamed at him that they needed to post a few officers around the forest to make sure the cult didn't try to sacrifice another person, and Vince had talked to the Chief about it, but he said there weren't enough reserve officers for a pointless task.

Vince had begun to wonder if the incompetence of the Tri-Cities police force was a new issue, or if it had always been lacking. Perhaps he and his partner had always been self-sufficient enough to never notice, or possibly the lack of anything drastic happening had made them soft. Either way, Vince was realizing help wasn't coming, and it was up to him and Lew to solve this problem.

After his enlightening chat with the Chief, Vince had decided to do a little research on the Wendigo. It was all bogus, of course, but if the cult believed this being was their master, he figured whatever he could learn about it would help to crawl inside their heads and determine their motivation.

The Wendigo was a mythological creature first referred to by First Nations tribes of Canada and the Americas. Many tribes had words that referenced The Wendigo, including the Ojibwe, the Naskapi, the Innu, and the Cree. Vince was fairly certain there were some Cree descendants still living on the protected lands just outside city limits. He made a note to talk to someone who might know about their historical lore.

Outside of fictional stories, there wasn't a whole lot of information regarding the Wendigo online, but the one recurring theme that jumped out at Vince was the idea of cannibalism. That coupled with excessiveness fit within the parameters of what had already happened in Angel's Rest. According to legend the Wendigo was simultaneously gluttonous and withering away. This had to do with the idea that when it ate a human it would grow in proportion to the one it ate, which would leave it constantly in a state of starvation, needing more to try and fill the void.

The descriptions of the Wendigo sent waves of chills through Vince, and a whole slew of questions came to him, including next steps to take and possible leads to follow. One of these leads meant calling up his ex who was a clinical psychologist. If he knew of anyone else with such a wide range of topical knowledge within psychology, he would gladly approach them, but he really didn't have any options.

He had grabbed a pen, written down a list of to-dos and, when he was semi-satisfied with his list, sat back in his chair and stared. His brain was reeling, and he didn't want to believe anything that was happening, but he had seen with his own eyes what these people were capable of, and he wasn't about to let it continue.

After what seemed like an eternity, he stood up, took a deep breath, and steeled himself the call with his ex-wife. They weren't enemies by any stretch, but he never felt comfortable when her clinical eye was on him.

However, delaying the inevitable would only serve to put him further behind the situation, so he resolved himself to his fate and left his office.

3

A metronome ticked monotonously on Jane's desk. The sound made Vince want to throw something across the room. He was aware that people often found comfort in the consistency of a metronome, but to him it was like someone dragging fingernails across a chalkboard; to him it was a subtle taunt at his self-control.

The door to his ex-wife's office opened and she stepped inside, sighing deeply at the sight of Vince. Vince's shoulders tensed and he forced himself to stare straight ahead until Jane was seated behind her desk.

He could feel her playing the game along with him, and after a long moment she made the decision to sit. She tented her fingers and smiled at him, but Vince could swear he felt the condescension in the slight upraise of her lips.

"Hello, Vincent. My assistant says that you could use my help with a case you're working on." She cocked her head slightly, in a gesture Vince knew all too well as her enjoying the bit of power she had over him in the moment.

"Jane, please, I'd like to ask you a few questions and get out of your hair. I know you don't want me here. I don't want to be here. But I'm stuck. We are experiencing some weird happenings, and they make no sense." Vince felt himself rambling but couldn't help it. She had always known the triggers to set him on edge.

Jane raised her hands and nodded slowly. "I am all ears. Please, Vincent, ask any question you need, and I will do my best to assist you."

Vince took a deep breath, never taking his eyes off the woman sitting across from him. Looking at her reminded him of why he loved her so much, but also why they never quite got along enough to make it last.

"There seems to be a cult that has moved into Angel's Rest. It started with one guy we found surrounded by the corpses of countless animals that he had ingested raw. And then we found a guy tacked to a tree, some of his internal organs removed."

He paused, knowing the next piece of the puzzle would either make Jane laugh or roll her eyes.

"I brought the first guy in for interrogation, because it felt like there was a connection. I had a gut feeling."

As he spoke, he marveled at how Jane was the only person with whom he felt the need to defend himself. He came to her for help, but here he was justifying his actions as a Detective.

"Your gut feelings have always been fairly accurate," Jane said with a kind smile. Vince waited. "Unless you have been drinking excessively again. Then your gut..." she allowed the rest of the thought to trail off into the ether.

Vince felt the color rising up his neck and fought to control his emotions.

"Anyway, I brought this guy Martin into the station and nothing I said to him had any effect. Until I mentioned mushrooms in the forest. I had gone out to the forest after the first incident and fell into a patch of mushrooms and ended up hallucinating, so I was curious if he may have experienced the same thing." Always justifying his actions to her.

"Hallucinogens have been known to help people with pronounced PTSD along with a whole host of other ailments. And it's becoming more accepted within the field of psychology. Have you had a drink since your encounter with the psilocybin?" She leaned back in her chair and peered at him intently.

Vince looked away, trying to remember if he had drunk anything since the incident, but couldn't recall. "I'm not sure, but I don't think so. I've had a lot on my plate, a lot on my mind. I don't really have time to drink right now."

Jane nodded her head. "That could be a side effect of the psilocybin. I would caution you that sometimes one addiction can be replaced with another very easily."

Vince thought about that for a moment, and then snapped out of his own thoughts. He glared at Jane and pointed an accusatory finger at her. "Hey, we are not here to psychoanalyze me. That's not why I came. Stop trying to get inside my head."

Jane clucked her tongue, which reminded Vince of the metronome, and he felt the anger rise inside of his chest. "Vincent, Vincent, Vincent. You come to me for help. You give me details. And when I try to help you understand what might be happening, you bite my head off. I don't appreciate it, and I think we might be done here."

Vince rose before Jane could and held out a staying hand. "No, please. I'm sorry. You're right. Let me just finish telling you what I came to tell you and hopefully you can help. Okay?"

Jane nodded and Vince sat back in his chair. "When I mentioned the mushrooms to Martin, he immediately became alert and interested in our conversation. He was leaving the room but turned to me with an intense look on his face." Vince knew he was stalling, but the whole idea still seemed ridiculous in his own head.

"He asked me if I had met the Wendigo." It was out. He had voiced the issue and now could only silently wait for Jane to laugh in his face.

"Based on what you have told me so far, that actually makes a lot of sense," Jane said, no trace of irony or sarcasm in her voice.

"It makes sense? How?" Vince felt as if he were now defending himself from his own question.

"There is a mental issue that is exceedingly rare but does exist known as Wendigo syndrome or Wendigo psychosis. It causes the individual to act out in a cannibalistic manner. And very aggressively. The ingesting of animals, the ritualistic pinning with organs missing, these point to someone who has a cannibalistic bent. This person, Martin, if he is behind the murder, is probably extremely unwell. Mentally."

"Would someone with this psychosis be able to function normally outside of the proclivity toward eating other people?" Vince was relieved that she was taking the idea seriously, and already felt one step closer to solving the case.

"For the most part they would seem no different than any other normal person. If their hunger reached a boiling point, they might abandon all reason to satiate the obsession. But fairly normal outside of that." Jane had gone into full teaching mode and Vince was reminded again why he had loved her so dearly.

"Now, there are also fetishes that involve cannibalism. It is a subculture within BDSM that isn't talked about a lot, mainly because of the taboo nature of the desire to eat another human's flesh, but it *does* exist. What you are talking about though fits more directly into the syndrome or psychosis."

She paused, collecting her thoughts. Vince saw her gearing up to ask a question, and he knew it was going to be directed at him. He steeled himself in an attempt to receive the question without defense.

"I have to ask you this, Vincent. And I don't want you to get defensive. This is a probing question to try and help you narrow down whatever is happening."

She waited until he nodded to proceed. "Have you felt any cannibalistic urges since you fell into the mushrooms?"

Vince bit his tongue, trying to remain calm. He knew the question was a smart one to ask, but the shame associated with the idea of cannibalism caused his head to spin. He knew the answer, but to be asked this felt like being asked if he ever hurt a child.

He took a deep breath before responding and found that the line of reasoning was clear as day and incredibly insightful. "I have not had any notions toward cannibalism. You think maybe a side effect of the mushrooms could exacerbate the psychosis?"

"It's possible. Have you sent the fungi in for testing?"

"I have. I should hear back hopefully by tomorrow."

All trepidation of this meeting fell away and both Vince and Jane fell into a rhythm of question and response, sculpting the story as best they could to help solve the mystery.

"That's good. I have done a little research into the Wendigo, and I believe there is a tribe of plains Cree a little way outside of the Tri-Cities on a reservation. They're one of the tribes who subscribed to the folklore. I doubt you will find any believers anymore, but First Nations traditions and lore are especially important, so I'm sure you will find someone who is at least knowledgeable on the topic."

"I was going to talk to a historian, but I will probably start with the reservation. If the tales of the Wendigo have been passed down, it's like cutting out the middleman. I'll see about visiting them tomorrow."

"If I think of anything else, I'll shoot you an email. Hopefully, you can stop this before it turns into a serial situation. I know if anyone is capable, you are."

Vince was stunned by the compliment. For a second, he was unable to articulate any further thoughts, but he finally was able to get a few words out. "I hope so too."

Vince stood to leave, and Jane stood too. "Vince, please be careful.

I..." she looked away and didn't finish the thought.

He reached out and squeezed her shoulder and smiled. "I don't plan on making anyone attend a funeral dedicated to me for a long time."

Jane simply nodded and Vince felt a strong wave of affection. He wanted her to hold him and to tell her he had an ominous feeling about the whole situation. But he knew the dangers in going down that path. And Jane would remind him of the dangers of developing feelings while in the middle of a stressful situation. The hormones that were affected in the body that falsely transmitted a desire for intimacy with the other person involved. So, he did the only thing he could think of and walked silently and quickly out of Jane's office, leaving her standing behind her desk, alone.

4

Lew stared up at Vince with a goofy grin on his face. He allowed the awkwardness to grow until Vince shifted from one foot to the other and let out a small cough. Then he spoke, "How was it seeing her again? You find it a bit hard?"

Vince glared at Lew, wanting to wipe the cheeky smile off his face. "It was fine. She was actually quite helpful. Confirmed my suspicions on a lead I'm going to follow up on tomorrow."

Seeing that Vince wasn't going to take the bait, Lew sobered up and asked, "What lead?"

"I'm going up to the land of the plains Cree. It's about 40 miles outside of town. I assume someone on the reservation will have some knowledge of the Wendigo. It's worth a shot." Vince chewed on the inside of his cheek, plotting the next day in his head.

"What if another person turns up while you're gone?" Lew raised his eyebrows.

Vince shrugged and replied, "I'm sure they can handle it." He let out a long sigh, "Besides, I'm really hoping for a small break from the carnage. Maybe I can will it to happen."

Lew let out a short laugh. "Wouldn't that be nice. Perhaps we can will the unsubs to turn themselves in while we're at it."

"Shut up, Lew," Vince said without any real conviction.

"Okay, so tomorrow you go up to the Cree res, hope to get a bit more information on the Wendigo, and I sit on my thumb. This is getting annoying."

"I need you to follow our friend, Martin. If he is involved in all this as deeply as I suspect, he'll be in preparation mode."

Lew looked up at Vince and replied, "I already checked. He's working all day tomorrow." He paused, waiting for a reaction, but Vince remained silent. "I guess I could stake him out. Couldn't hurt. What else am I gonna do?"

Vince closed his eyes and rubbed a hand over his face. "I know. But it is what it is. And I feel like we're working well within the parameters we have been forced into."

Lew nodded but stayed silent.

Vince could see the inability to work on much wearing on Lew, and he knew he would be the same if he were on that side of the table. There was this bug inside of detectives that itched whenever there was some mystery, and they were unable to solve it. He had seen a few detectives who were unable to shake the bug and it drove them crazy. They lost their edge and spiraled until they were unable to trust their own judgment on the job. Detective burn out.

There were plenty of regular people who had the itch as well, but when it was in the job description to figure it all out it burned that much brighter. And Vince felt like they were caught in a loop, which was not uncommon for detective work. A lead pops up and is followed in a full circle until another lead pops up and the cycle repeats. The feeling of not accomplishing anything had been known to rankle even the most immovable detectives.

Vince remembered talking to a detective once who had a far-off stare no matter what they were discussing. It could have been a cold case or who won the World Series, it didn't matter. They had been at a diner, and the other man had sat with his food in front of him for nearly an hour and hadn't touched it.

At one point he had looked directly at Vince, but Vince could tell he was looking through him to somewhere in the distance. The detective said, "When the itch isn't able to be scratched, you find yourself questioning everything. Did you log the evidence? Did you really see the small blood spatter on the windowsill or was it simply a trick of the light? Are the officers laughing behind your back, calling you senile and suggesting you land in a retirement facility? It eats at you. It gnaws at your reason and sanity. And there isn't a damn thing you can do about it."

He had rolled up one of his sleeves and Vince could see scratch marks on his arm. And there were scars underneath the fresh scratches.

The detective continued, "And you know, deep down, that there is nothing physically there. That no matter how far down you try to dig into your own body you will find no relief. But it doesn't matter anymore. So, you dig. And you search. And you doubt."

For the first, and only time during that meal, the detective actually stared directly at Vince, seeing him, acknowledging him. Vince saw the tears pooling at the corners of his eyes and the man said, "And then you fizzle and die. There is no reasoning left. Nothing makes sense." The detective wiped at his eyes. "Nothing but the itch."

And he stood up from the table and left.

Vince had monitored local news where the detective lived for nearly a year after that, waiting to hear how he had committed suicide, but the only thing he ever saw was when the detective retired from the police force in the middle of a case; a case they never ended up solving.

With a sigh, Vince focused back onto Lew and said, "Promise me that if you see me start to lose it you'll help me. I don't want to burn out over this case. Can you do that for me?"

Lew leaned toward Vince, concern creeping into his voice as he replied, "I won't let that happen to you. I promise. I'm on the outside. I've got a different perspective. We'll run this thing by the numbers and become local heroes once again and laugh about it over a bucket of beers."

Vince nodded his head, feeling an itch deep inside his stomach; an itch he couldn't quite scratch. A wave of fear washed over him and then was gone. He smiled at Lew but felt the unease worming its way inside his head. If they didn't solve this case soon, he was afraid he would lose himself. He couldn't let that happen.

SEPTEMBER 18

1

The drive took Vince longer than he had anticipated, partly due to the fact that his 40 miles outside of town notion had ended up being closer to 80, and partly because there had been a gruesome accident on the Interstate that had slowed traffic to a crawl. But seeing as how this was the only lead on his agenda for the day, he didn't mind the bit of isolation.

He had felt a weight lift off of him as soon as he had left the city limits. It was almost as if the city itself was under an oppressive darkness; existing in its own bubble where gravity had increased tenfold and anyone looking in from the outside wouldn't be able to feel it.

Now he was on a dirt road, heading deep into the Cree reservation, and he was enjoying the view. The res itself was simple, nothing ostentatious about it, but Vince knew they were self-sustaining and had everything they needed to keep to themselves, from fruit to Wi-Fi.

The house he was now heading toward was owned by a gentleman named George Saunders. George was born on the reservation and had lived there his entire life. And everyone in town had immediately pegged him as the historian who would likely know more about the legend of the Wendigo.

Vince had been driving beneath a nice shade of pine trees, but as they thinned, a seemingly endless plain was left in its place. As far as he could see it was flat, with small brush and leafless trees dotting the landscape. It was barren and yet serene. Vince felt that if he didn't focus on the task, he would forget his reason for coming.

He finally arrived at a modest cabin, smoke trickling out a brick chimney. A man sat on a rocking chair on the front porch, delicately whittling with a bone handled knife. He didn't look up as the detective approached and Vince figured it either meant he was expected, or the man had a shotgun at the ready to emphasize his disdain for the intrusion.

Vince parked and exited his vehicle, making sure his service piece was properly attached to his person. He felt the crunch of the pea gravel under his feet as he made his way toward the man on the porch. Finally, when he was within the range of being heard at a normal tone, Vince called out, "Are you George?"

The man continued to whittle. "Could be."

Vince nodded. "Good enough." He didn't know if he should mount the stairs and try and shake the man's hand or stay where he was, so he said, "I hear you are the town historian. You've been here your whole life." He paused briefly and then added, "If you *are* George Saunders, that is."

Vince thought he saw a little smile play at the corner of the man's mouth, but it could have been a trick of the day's lengthening light.

Finally, the man put his knife down and leaned back, rocking slowly. "Suppose I am George. And suppose I am an historian. Why would that concern you?"

"I'm just trying to get some information on some folklore passed down by your ancestors." Vince was starting to feel as though the man was toying with him.

"The Wendigo, huh?" The man stopped rocking and leaned forward, getting a closer look at Vince.

Vince smiled warmly and replied, "Word travels fast. It's nice to meet you, George. People in town seem to have every confidence in your knowledge."

George stood up and walked down to meet Vince. They shook

hands and George patted Vince on the shoulder. "I gotta feed my cows. Care to join me?"

Before Vince could reply, George was walking past him. "My name is Vincent. Vince. Detective Aronson."

George smiled as he walked. "Well, Vincent Vince Detective Aronson, that is quite the mouthful, but we'll make do."

Vince felt his face go red. "You can call me Vince. So, George, how many cows do you…" his voice trailed off as he looked out at a large field filled with nearly 300 cows.

George waved the question away as he replied, "Just a couple. No big deal," and continued to walk toward the herd.

"A couple. Yeah, well…" Vince found himself at a loss, his brain attempting to keep up with the nonchalant nature of the man before him.

"But you didn't come all the way out here to talk cows. Ask me your questions. I am a terribly busy man."

They approached the fence, which was simply a few wires at different heights strung between posts. "These wires keep the cows in? Fascinating."

Vince reached out for the fence, but George slapped the back of his hand. "I wouldn't touch that. First jolt feels like one of those novelty buzzer toys. By the third jolt your whole body would be tingling."

A look of understanding passed between the two men. "Electrified. Got it."

George moved off toward a barn and some of the cows followed along with them as they walked. "Do you remember when I told you I was busy?" George looked over at Vince out of the corner of his eye.

"Yeah. Sorry. The Wendigo. How much do you know about it?" Vince found that he had to focus intently on what George was saying or he got swept up in looking at all the cows.

George shrugged. "I know some. Sara knows more. I'll tell you what I can though."

They came to the barn and George rolled back one of the giant doors as if it were made of particle board. "The Wendigo folklore came about when a bunch of tribes were going through an extremely harsh winter. People turned on each other and it looked like a sickness was afflicting them. But this wasn't a physical illness, it was more psychological. They panicked and started to eat each other.

"The elders got together and came up with a plan to create the Wendigo as a symbol for what starvation and greed can do to a person. After the first tribesperson ate another, they had the doctor declare that if someone was infected, they were to be quarantined until it passed. They came up with the Wendigo idea to scare people away from cannibalism.

"If the people believed that some spiritual being was making them feel this way, maybe they could try and fight it." George stepped over to a simple wooden bench and pointed to a corner of the barn. "Would you mind bringing me that stack of buckets over there?"

Vince moved off to grab the buckets and asked, "And did that stop the cannibalistic tendencies?"

He handed the buckets to George who then pointed behind him and said, "Grab a bench and park it beside me."

Vince did as he was told, patiently waiting for his question to be answered. But George remained silent, going through his routine before the cows started filing into the barn.

George looked over at Vince. "You ever milk a cow before, Vince?"

Vince shrugged. "Probably at a dairy farm on a field trip in junior high. I don't really remember."

A cow approached George and turned so he had access to her udders. He grabbed a teat in each hand and squeezed and pulled until a fine stream of milk came out, landing in the metal bucket. "It's quite simple once you get the hang of it. Squeeze and pull, gentle but firm, and you will have a full bucket in no time."

A cow made its way in front of Vince, who swallowed loudly. "How in the world do you milk all these cows by hand? There's got to be about 300 of them."

"Three-hundred-forty-seven actually. And not all of them are milking cows. Actually, most *aren't* milking cows. I only have four females. This is a cattle farm, not a dairy farm, so most of the animals you saw will be used for meat and clothing. I would suggest not trying to milk one of them. So, you see, not all of them need to be milked every day."

Vince grabbed hold of one of the cow's teats and glanced over at George to confirm the motion. Once he was confident in his grip, he tried to produce some milk. At first none came out and the cow shifted uncomfortably. But after a few attempts he had the hang of it and the milk hitting the bucket was rhythmic with George's attempts.

George continued with his story. "It worked for a while. But the winter lasted so long and was so harsh, they started to become paranoid. Anyone who looked at another person was up for the nomination of cannibal. And children began telling others they had spotted the Wendigo in the trees. They had a game where they would stand as close to the forest as possible for as long as they could before running back home."

The cow Vince was working with gave a low moo and Vince realized no more milk was coming out. He released the cow and it walked away, only to be replaced by another. He looked down and noticed that there was no milk in the bucket, and his fingers and arms were already aching. A look of disappointment crossed his face as he shook his hands out and George laughed.

"You city boys and your smooth palms. It takes a while to get the hang of milking a cow. Besides, it does you good to do a hard day's work every now and then. Reminds you that there are others out in the world besides yourself. Puts a little gratitude in your heart."

Vince wanted to be offended, but George's demeanor was so matter of fact without a lick of condescension in his voice that he simply shrugged and started milking the next cow. He noticed that the cows he had been *milking* were becoming frustrated with his lack of experience and had been making their way over to George.

"The problem with legends," George continued, changing out his second full bucket, "is they grow in the mind. They become monstrous without proof. Have you ever played that game Telephone?"

"Where someone comes up with a phrase and you pass it down the line to see how accurate it is by the end?"

"That's the one. As legends pass down the line, they become larger and larger until they are godlike. If no one had ever laid eyes on a rabbit, the legend of the rabbit could become so distorted that by the time someone actually saw one they wouldn't know what the hell it was.

"We love our morality tales that help scare children enough to keep them in line, but if that's all they hear, reality becomes twisted. Children grow up afraid of anything they don't know."

"It becomes monstrous." Vince was making the connections now.

George put a finger to his nose. "Precisely. If we apply that to the Wendigo, we now see in our mind's eye a creature as tall as an evergreen and as emaciated as a picked apart carcass.

"The original concept was to show these tribes that greed was not sustainable. No matter how much you take and take you always want more. As humans we were made to share with one another. Some religions refer to it as communion or breaking bread together. The idea is to remain grateful for your bounty by sharing it with others. Not as a show of what you have—"

"But to show gratitude for the people who surround you as well." Vince finished the thought before realizing he had interrupted the older man. But when he looked over, George was smiling and nodding his head.

"You've caught the tail and are following it to the meat. You are a smart one Vincent Vince Detective Aronson." Vince's face flushed briefly.

He realized he hadn't asked any of the questions he had come to ask, but the knowledge he was gaining was invaluable.

"How much do you know about the Cree, Detective?"

"Not much. Mostly what I read on the Internet. You came from Canada and split into different tribes, some of which ended up down here in the states. And your tribe was one of the ones that passed along the legend of the Wendigo."

"Other than that, it seems you are fairly ignorant about us." Vince opened his mouth to protest, but George held up a hand. "Now don't get offended. The term ignorance has such a negative connotation, but it simply means lacking knowledge or understanding. I am ignorant in many things. That is why we educate ourselves. That is how we grow as humans. We become less ignorant by asking those who have the knowledge."

George sat up straight and rubbed the small of his back before continuing. "You are very receptive to learning and becoming less ignorant. That's the only reason you are still here talking with me. I don't have time for people who ask questions and have already filled the answers in their minds."

Vince looked down to see he still hadn't managed to succeed at getting anything into the bucket and he sighed. George chuckled and waited for the cow to approach him. Deftly, he milked the last cow in silence, Vince watching in awe.

After a couple minutes, George stood up and grabbed a pipe out of his shirt pocket. He packed it with a sweet-smelling tobacco and lit it. "Do you believe you would be a good detective if you had pre-formed answers in your head before asking your questions?"

Vince frowned and shook his head. "It would cause me to jump to conclusions. It would create false positives and I'd be out of a job. This is why I wanted to talk to someone who has a direct lineage of the legend of the Wendigo. I am…ignorant, and I want to educate myself by talking to someone who has the knowledge."

He wasn't used to not having an edge on the person he was talking to, but this man was so unassuming and confident in himself it was disarming. Vince found that he was unable to properly profile George because he was hiding nothing. What he saw before him was what everyone saw. He was genuinely himself.

Vince felt like George had opened the floor for his questioning to begin. "So, can we assume that the Wendigo is real for a moment?"

George nodded, letting a curl of smoke slowly exit his mouth.

"What could be done to stop such a creature? And why would it be here now?" Vince bit on his tongue, because the questions wanted to freely flow from him, but asking fourteen questions in a row would only confuse the situation.

"Well, are you familiar with Totem Poles?"

"Vaguely. I know they are significant in your culture, but that's about it."

"Totem Poles are a series of symbols of figures stacked one on the other. They can represent a myriad of ideas including territory, songs, dances, and spirits. With regards to the Totem Pole and the Wendigo, perhaps it could be bound by a Pole representing our spirit guides. Maybe that's why it hasn't made an appearance until now. It could very well have been restricted by Totems. Some cultures use cairns of stone as symbols."

Vince knew they were speaking purely in the hypothetical, but the passion underlining everything George was saying sent a chill down his spine. The man spoke as though he had encountered nefarious beings in his life that needed to be held at bay by various totems.

George snapped his fingers, startling Vince and the cow he was milking. "I wonder if someone destroyed the Totems. That could be why the Wendigo is rearing its ugly head now. Where did you say all of this was happening?"

"I didn't, but they are on the edge of the forest in Angel's Rest. We haven't ventured far into the woods because we haven't found the need."

"Binding the Wendigo in the forest is not ideal, but it may have been their only choice at the time. The Wendigo is able to hide amongst the trees easily. Someone not paying attention could possibly even walk right by it without noticing its presence." George looked down and saw that Vince's last bucket was full. "I will send my grandson to collect the buckets. We must talk to Sara about this."

Without another word George exited the barn and Vince had to scurry out behind him before George closed the door on him. He was starting to wonder if George really believed the Wendigo existed or if he simply wanted to send him away fully educated on the legend.

2

Sara sat in front of a wood stove, her head slumped but rising and falling with each breath. George knelt slowly beside her and gently rubbed her face with the back of his hand. "Auntie Sara, I have someone here I'd like you to talk to."

It took her a moment to rouse herself from her slumber, and when she did, she looked at George and smiled. "Georgie, how good to see you. How was your day?"

"It was very fine, Auntie." He gestured at Vince. "This is Vincent. He's a detective from the Tri-Cities. He would like to talk to you about a case he's working on, if you are up for that."

Sara took George's hand in hers and patted it with her other hand. "Anything for you, my dear. I am strong as an ox still. You know this."

George smiled and nodded. Sara turned to Vince, and he could see that she was quite old, but there was still a sparkle in her eye. She was an extraordinarily strong person. She reached out her hands toward Vince. "Take my hands, young man. Let us connect as we speak to one another."

Without hesitation Vince held out his hands and felt her warmth radiate through his body. She nodded slightly, inviting Vince to start the conversation.

Vince took a deep breath and began, "Miss Sara, I am working on a case right now where some people believe they have encountered a Wendigo."

Sara's hands briefly tightened but relaxed just as quickly. "I haven't spoken of the Wendigo in many years. The last of those who claimed to have encountered one during their lifetime passed on around thirty years ago."

Vince glanced at George, but George's attention was fully on Sara. She spoke of the Wendigo as if they were discussing plans for the coming Sunday. The sincerity in Sara's voice captivated him and he nodded for her to continue.

"Of course, growing up we heard the tale of the Wendigo. The curse of greed and wanton desire. But all cultures have their tales to help people remain on a virtuous path." She smiled warmly at Vince.

"Is it possible that this Wendigo could exist? That these people really *have* encountered a creature out in the forest?" Vince was beginning to feel as though his instincts were faltering. If George and Sara believed that the Wendigo was simply a story passed down, maybe he was going about this whole investigation wrong. He should focus on Martin and his connection to the cult. Maybe by singling him out he could finally make headway on his investigation.

Sara squeezed his hands slightly again, bringing him back to the present. "There are a lot of things that people believe, but whether the manifestation of their belief is a physical reality, or a metaphysical concept is often determined by that individual."

"So, these people could be seeing what they want to see. Conjuring up an image and idea in their heads to conform to their hopes." It was more of a musing than a question.

"More to conform to their needs. What is it someone needs that would make them turn to the idea of the Wendigo? Do they feel the world owes them something they are not receiving? Is there a part of them that wishes they could be justified in acting out the depravity that lies within their minds? It's difficult to tell. Just because something isn't able to be touched, tasted, smelled doesn't mean it isn't real in one sense or another." Sara looked a bit winded, but when she noticed George take a step toward her, she waved him off.

Sara continued, "Every action has an equal and opposite reaction.

Likewise, every belief system has an opposing force that pushes back against it equally. Heaven and hell. Yin and Yang. Good versus evil. Yahweh and the devil. They are inevitably bound to one another. And because of that there is always a way to suppress either side. You could embrace the light and the darkness fades, or you could move toward darkness and the light dims."

Vince bit the inside of his lip. What she was saying rang true. But he felt it wasn't always so cut and dry. Her example of Yin and Yang incorporated bits of darkness into the light and vice versa. Nonetheless, the struggle between two sides was universal.

Finally, after a long silence, he said, "So, if these people believe the Wendigo is real, all I would have to do to end it would be to destroy the Wendigo. If the object of their obsession is destroyed, they can no longer subscribe to the notion."

Sara smiled and gave Vince a look that indicated he was partially correct with his statement. "Even destroyed, something can be clung to. It is human nature to hold onto a belief. Without the ability to believe in something, nihilism winds its way into the heart."

"Nothing and nobody truly matter," Vince said in a near whisper. "How do I convince these people that if they continue along their path, it will only leave others hurt or dead? How do I stop them?"

"If they genuinely believe this Wendigo is making a reentry into the world, where he will prosper and become more powerful, you must find a way to bind it, and keep it where it can do no harm. That is my suggestion to you." Sara stared intently at Vince, a look of compassion and infinite knowledge on her face.

She squeezed his hands once more and whispered, "The devils of this world may exist differently than we imagine, so we must keep moving forward with open hearts and open minds," and with that last bit of effort Sara laid her head back down on her chest and fell asleep.

Vince looked over at George who looked concerned. Vince wasn't sure if the look was for Sara or regarding the topic of discussion. The chill returned to Vince's spine as he asked, "This *is* still only a hypothetical. Right?"

George looked directly into Vince's eyes and replied, "Let's hope so. I'll walk you out."

3

Vince's thoughts clicked together rhythmically, ping-ponging from one idea to another. It reminded him of the metronome in Jane's office, and he turned on the radio to drown out the sound of his own musings.

He didn't really want to take any stock in the concept of the Wendigo being an actual entity, but perhaps these cultists were followers of the mythos, so they were willing to play out the fantastical portions of what it might entail to be in the trusted circle of the beast. And to that end, he wasn't sure if he was more frightened of the belief of the Wendigo by these believers, or the possibility of the Wendigo itself.

The effects of fanaticism had woven their way into the bedrock of societies throughout history. If left unchecked for long enough it soon became the norm. The hope here was to nip the bud early enough to keep it from blooming into a full-fledged movement.

Vince realized the monotony of his thoughts was slowly lulling him to sleep. He sat up and smacked himself on the cheeks a couple times, clearing his throat and opening his eyes wide. Reaching into his pocket he grabbed his cell phone and quick dialed Lew. He figured he may as well update him on the new bits of information that had come to light.

Lew picked up on the second ring, sounding out of breath. "What's up, buddy?"

"You running from something?"

"Just my commitments. You got some juicy gossip to share with me?" Lew's breathing slowed and Vince envied how quickly he could recover and return to normalcy.

"I went up to the reservation today and had a lovely chat with a couple of the locals. They helped me to understand a bit more of the mythology behind the Wendigo. It didn't seem like anyone really believed in an actual being, but there was still a bit of reverence when they spoke about it."

Lew let out a low whistle. "Crazy. The power of tradition, I guess."

Vince thought about that for a moment before responding, "The thing is, the old lady, Sara, had a hint of fear in her eyes when she talked about it. Almost as if she had lived through something like this before. She told me one way to stop this cult would be to bind the hypothetical Wendigo to keep it from escaping."

"Escaping? Where does this hypothetical it want to go?"

"Back into the world. The power of belief could sweep through the Tri-Cities, building on the claims of the occultists."

"Unless we trap it again."

"Unless we trap it again," Vince agreed. "But what if there is something real behind all of this? What if the Wendigo is an actual being? My tuning fork is all out of whack here, partner. I feel like I'm swimming in a pitch-black sea and can't find my way to the surface. The thought that the Wendigo might exist terrifies me.

Lew barked a laugh and added, "Why are we talking about this like it's real?"

Vince thought about it for a long moment before responding. "Because if we don't treat it like it's real, we have nowhere else to go if nothing else fits. I'm not saying we go out of our way to try and find the Wendigo, but if we find ourselves on an island without a way off, it's a contingency plan."

"You're going out to the forest to try and find this place, aren't you?"

Vince uttered a humorless laugh. "Due diligence, my dear Lewis. Due diligence."

"Let me pack my gear and we can make a day of it. Exploring the woods like kids again."

A hint of excitement entered Lew's voice, and Vince wondered if his partner wasn't getting a little anxious with nothing to do but wait for the daily report and tail Martin.

"Lew, I would love for you to come with me, but think of it from the other side." Vince knew Lew would figure it out, so he let it hang in the air for a minute.

Finally, Lew responded. "Oh, come on. There's nothing out there. It's like a long hike. That's all."

"And if something happens to me, I need you to be able to come and find me."

"I don't like this, Vince."

"You're just bored."

There was a long silence from the other end of the line. Then, "Maybe. I mean, Martin has done absolutely nothing. Nothing."

Vince sighed. "I'm going to need you to track my phone's GPS, and if I'm not back before nightfall, come in and get me. I will take my gun and plenty of snacks."

He heard a slight chuckle from Lew's side and relaxed a bit. "I was mostly worried about your food intake. But this is some horror movie level stupidity. *Hey, let's split up and meet later.*"

"Except this is real life and we're detectives. We have training. And if there actually is something in the woods it'll probably be a bear or mountain lion. Nothing I can't handle."

Vince was sure his voice sounded calm and confident, but on the inside, he was feeling the first tendrils of panic creeping into his chest. The doubts began flashing through his head.

"And he was never heard from again."

"Not gonna happen."

"That's what they all say," Lew scoffed, which sent a slight twinge of irritation through Vince's body.

"Any more cliches you want to pile on before you're done?"

Lew must have heard the frustration in his voice because he immediately softened his tone. "You don't get to tell me not to worry about you. That's not your call. You are my friend. And I'd be super bored if you bit the bullet."

The tension broke and they both laughed. Vince wiped his eyes, glad to have someone who actually cared about him before traipsing into the woods all by his lonesome.

"I'll let you know when I enter the forest, and I'll try and send an *all-good* text every couple hours. Deal?"

"Deal. Don't get yourself killed out there."

"Promise." Vince took a deep breath, doubt already trying to find a home within him.

He ended the call and sat in silence, hoping he was making the right decision. Hoping he wasn't wasting a whole day with an empty pursuit. And most of all, hoping he didn't run into the Wendigo.

SEPTEMBER 19

1

Birds chirped in the early morning sun, but to Vince it felt like a false sense of security. The ominous pit from the day before had dropped from his chest into his stomach. He hadn't brought much with him because he certainly didn't anticipate finding anything of note in the woods. He was out here for a brisk walk and nothing else.

He tried to convince himself that the reason for the hesitation was because he didn't want to find another body tacked to a tree, but deep inside he knew that was surface level at best. It was a shame that he had come to dislike the forest, because he knew it could truly be a peaceful place.

He grabbed his cell phone and sent a quick text to Lew letting him know his journey was about to begin. With a deep breath, he cinched his travel pack tighter and stepped across the threshold into the mass of trees.

For a time he followed the widest and most worn path, ignoring the side paths and overgrown areas. He figured if he stayed on what appeared to be the most well-worn trail, he would then be able to track the smaller ones without getting lost. Once he was satisfied he had traversed most of the main path he would then make his way back, checking side trails as he went.

It took him nearly an hour until he came to a large juncture where paths branched off almost like spokes on a wagon wheel. He counted eight separate ways he could go, and a few of the trails were as wide and well-worn as the one he was on. As long as he could find his way back to one of the large trails, he was sure he could easily find his way out of the forest, even if it was not to the exact point he had entered. Besides the fact that he had downloaded a GPS app that showed him exact longitude and latitude and he had marked his insertion point with a virtual pin.

Vince had all his bases covered, so he decided to start veering off the main path in hopes of finding something worth his time.

One of the paths was almost completely overgrown with grass and ferns and he picked his way along carefully, trying to avoid any potential poison oak that might be lurking to make someone's life a living hell. This he knew from experience.

He had only been walking for a few minutes when he came to another wagon wheel intersection. This one only broke off onto even smaller paths. As he turned to make his way back to the main trail, he noticed multiple options heading back in the general direction from where he had come. He was fairly certain he knew the trail he had taken to get to this point, so he began to retrace his steps.

As he walked, he checked his GPS app, and sure enough, the app was tracking every movement he made, so even if he did get himself lost, he wouldn't actually be lost.

After another ten minutes, Vince checked his app again and this time was startled to discover that he was now off the main trail and on another heading deeper into the woods. A moment of panic stung him, but he took a few deep breaths and slowed his heart rate so he could think clearly.

Obviously, he had taken a slightly different track from the first wagon wheel intersection, and now all he had to do was follow the GPS back along the route he had already taken, and he would be on course again. He checked his watch and saw there were a couple hours left before noon, still plenty of time to explore before heading home.

Watching his phone out of the corner of his eye, he carefully made his way back to the first intersection and placed another pin on the map. Relief flooded him. He hadn't wanted to admit it, but a small part of him was afraid he would get himself lost in the woods and never be able to find his way back. A text popped up on his screen:

You out there walking in circles? Your map looks like a damn dog trying to remember where he buried a bone. Hope you find what you're looking for. I'm gonna go eat a sandwich.

Vince laughed to himself and sent a quick response text before choosing another path to walk along.

This time he kept a closer eye on his phone and after walking another fifteen minutes ran across another intersection. Looking around, he could see more intersecting paths veering off from other paths and he wondered briefly how many people had come out here unprepared and had wound up lost in these woods forever.

A shiver found its way up his spine, and he pushed the thought away. He needed to focus if he was going to get anything done. He had looked up Angel's Rest Forest online and although it was quite small for a national forest it was still nearly 35,000 acres large. Plenty of room for someone to get lost. It was large enough for a few thousand people to get lost and never run into each other.

He looked at his phone again and saw that it was nearly two o'clock in the afternoon. But that made no sense. There was no way he had been walking for nearly five hours already. Vince scratched his head, confused.

When he looked down at his phone it showed a lot more lines than what he last remembered seeing. Had he been wandering long enough that he had lost track of time and distance? Nothing was making sense. He looked around and saw all the paths around him he had seen before. Something wasn't adding up.

He saw where he was on the GPS and noticed he had been on a

single path for quite some time, but the last time he had checked he had only been on the path for about fifteen minutes. And he was certain he hadn't moved. His head hurt.

Something was terribly wrong, and he made the decision to head back toward his car. He would gather a team tomorrow to come out and comb the woods for any signs of disturbances. That is probably what he should have done in the first place. He saw his originating pin placement and saw a path heading in that direction. It wasn't the path he had come in on, but it would take him closer to his car, and there were so many intersecting trails he was bound to find his way back onto the main one eventually.

2

Time slipped past Vince unnoticed, and the sun was angled to the west before he knew what was happening. Sweat glistened on his brow and when he checked his phone, he was no closer to his car than when he started walking. The time was nearing four o'clock and the feeling of panic was rising in him again.

It was beginning to feel like a familiar friend. He imagined himself walking on a treadmill. The illusion of making progress was real, but his GPS told a different story. The first shadows of night began creeping into the edges of his vision. His pace quickened, as did his breathing.

And then something snapped inside his mind, and he began to run. He ran blindly, chasing trails that appeared out of the corner of his eye, hoping to catch a glimpse of the main trail that had brought him through the forest. Instead, he found more and more trails, leading off in different directions, an endless maze of dirt and dust.

By the time his wits had somewhat returned to him, he was out of breath and covered in a fine layer of forest floor. Sweat tracked down his face through the dirt and he was afraid tears weren't far behind. He doubled over, placing his hands on his knees, trying to calm his mind before it betrayed him again.

He stood up, taking in his surroundings. Nothing looked familiar, but everything looked the same. Vince checked his phone to find that it had run out of battery sometime during his panicked run. Scolding himself, he sat down hard onto the ground, letting the dust puff up around him, not caring that it was getting in his eyes and ears and mouth.

There was nothing left for him to do but blindly grope his way along the paths and hope they led him to some edge of the forest. He still had water and food, so he wouldn't starve or become dehydrated yet.

Now that he was calmer, he thought through the situation. The rule of thumb when you were lost was to stay where you were and wait for someone to find you. That was a great thought, except Lew was the only one who knew he was out there, and Vince had no idea the last time his movements were able to be tracked.

If he walked along the paths, hoping to find a way out, he could end up pushing himself deeper into the woods, and with night approaching, that would put him at risk of wildlife taking advantage of his vulnerability. He had his service pistol, but he hadn't packed any spare magazines, which meant he could take out a couple animals, but then would be defenseless.

The only other thing he could think to do was start yelling. Yell as loud as he was able and hope someone heard him. Pray he was close enough to the edge of the forest for anyone to be able to respond so he could follow their voice to safety.

He opened his mouth to yell, but the dirt had dried out his throat. Grabbing his water bottle, he dumped a bit over his head to cool himself down and then swished some in his mouth and spat it on the ground. Having done that, he took one giant gulp of water, feeling his throat clear up as he did. Inhaling deeply, he opened his mouth to yell as loud as he could, but before he could vocalize anything, he heard a small voice call out near him.

"Hello? Is someone there?"

3

Vince stopped dead in his tracks. He wasn't sure if he had actually heard a voice or if his panic had set off an auditory hallucination. All he could hear now was the rasping sound of his own breathing. Inhaling slowly, he held his breath in an attempt to hear anything else that would mesh the voice with reality.

After nearly a minute with only the sound of the wind sighing through the branches, he released his breath and tried a tentative, "Hello?" not expecting to hear any response.

A few more moments passed, and Vince was about to start walking again when he thought he heard a sniffling sound. Then the voice called out again. "Is someone there? I think I'm lost."

Vince moved to action immediately, heading toward the voice. It sounded like a young girl, and she had sounded badly frightened. "Yes, I'm here. My name is Detective Vincent Aronson. Follow the sound of my voice and I'll help you find your way home."

A rustling in the bushes to Vince's left awakened his instincts and his hand subconsciously made its way to the gun in its holster. He took a deep breath and relaxed his hand, hoping the child hadn't seen his nerves get the better of him.

The young girl emerged from the bush a moment later, covered in dirt, tracks of spent tears clearing a path through the dust on her cheeks.

Vince lowered himself to one knee and smiled to the girl. "Hey there. How did you get yourself all the way out here?"

The little girl's eyes rimmed with tears, and she sat heavily onto the forest floor, putting her head in her hands and letting out a hitched breath that was a telltale sign of a deep cry. "I came out here with my parents and they said I needed to stay with them, but I didn't. I saw a bug. You know?"

She looked up at Vince for confirmation and he nodded his head slightly in agreement. "It wasn't like any other bug I had seen before. It had all these colors. It looked like a rainbow."

Vince listened to her talk about the bug, but his mind was elsewhere, afraid this little girl would find out his dark secret about being just as lost as her. He knew he needed to be the adult, so he pushed the fear away and sat down on the ground with her. "How old are you?"

"Seven and three quarters," she said, smiling sadly.

"Almost eight. That's a good age. And what is your name?" Vince could see that she was calming down and breathing more normally.

"Brittany. Brittany Moss. My dad says it's a fitting last name, because of all the people who had taken a lichen to me." She smiled her sad smile again.

Vince stared at the girl, trying to place a Moss family in the Tri-Cities, but nothing rang any bells. Brittany mistook his silence for not understanding the joke and said, "You know. Cuz moss is a lichen?"

Nodding his head, Vince said, "That's very clever. I bet your dad has all sorts of jokes, doesn't he?"

Brittany rolled her eyes. "Soooo many. He's silly."

Now that Brittany had calmed down, Vince felt it was time for them to figure a way out of the woods. He felt no less lost than he had the moment before he had heard her voice, but he knew that kids had a way with remembering things and had an innate sense of direction. Brittany had simply worked herself up and was unable to focus on her path of escape. Sort of mimicking his own predicament.

Vince patted the ground and said, "Okay, Brittany. I have to be totally honest with you. I think I'm lost too. I don't remember which path I took to get out here, but I believe that if we put our heads together, we'll find our way out in no time. Do you think we can do that?"

Brittany nodded her head again and said, "Yeah. Sounds good to me."

"Okay, the first thing we need to do is sit here for a minute and breathe. Maybe if we relax our brains, we'll remember something important about how we got out here." Vince closed his eyes and took deep breaths in through his nose and out through his pursed lips, creating an almost soundless whisper. He peeked at Brittany and saw she was following his lead.

The forest was rapidly darkening, and he knew it would be harder to find their way without any light, not to mention the possibility of wildlife celebrating the find of some easy prey.

After nearly five minutes of their meditative act, Brittany stood abruptly. She started dancing around, anxious to give some information. "I know how to get to the lots of paths. The last one I passed before I realized I was lost."

Vince stood and dusted the forest floor off. "That's great. You lead the way, and I'll be right behind you."

Without another word, Brittany turned on her heel and headed back into the depths of the forest. It took a considerable effort for Vince to keep up with her, and more than once he had to follow solely by sound because he lost sight of her.

After five minutes of walking, Vince stepped out into a clearing to find Brittany sitting on the ground on the verge of tears again. She had clutched the dirt of the path and rivulets of the stuff was flowing between her fingers.

Vince sat down with her and started his breathing exercises, talking to Brittany in between breaths. "So, we do it again. We calm ourselves down, open our minds, and wait for a clue to show itself."

"Is that what you do as a detective?" Brittany side-eyed him, not wanting to move her head.

"That is exactly what I do as a detective. Do you remember approximately which direction you came from when you arrived at this intersection?"

Brittany bit her lip and then her eyes widened. "I know it. Or near it. Over here."

She stood up abruptly and began walking down one of the paths, when she stopped as suddenly as she had begun, seemingly afraid to move.

"What's wrong, Brittany? Is it *not* the right path?"

Brittany shook her head and held out her right hand. "I'm just scared. It's getting dark. Can you hold my hand?"

Vince walked up to her and wordlessly took her hand. He felt a small jump of electricity between their palms and prayed it didn't foreshadow a storm on the horizon. That was the last thing they needed while lost in the woods.

Brittany started to walk pulling Vince out of his thoughts. He hoped her muscle memory set them on the right path, because he had no idea how deep they actually were.

Brittany talked while she picked her path carefully along the trail. "Do you have any kids?"

None that he knew of. "Nope. No kids of my own."

"Oh, cuz you're real good with helping me. I bet you'd make a good daddy." She tugged on his arm, taking an adjoining path.

Vince breathed a sigh of relief. The girl seemed to be remembering her way back to civilization. He relaxed into the cadence of the hike and answered her questions as she asked them.

"How many people have you arrested?"

"Too many to remember."

"Have you caught any really bad guys?"

"A few. But nothing too crazy."

"Did you always want to be a detective?"

"Ever since I was little. Probably around your age."

"Do you like being a detective?"

"For the most part. Sometimes it makes me sad. But a lot of times I like my job."

The girl stopped abruptly. Vince looked around, hoping she hadn't heard the sound of a wild animal. He squeezed her hand in what he hoped she interpreted as a comforting gesture. He saw her furrow her brow, the first gesture of confusion in a long while.

Vince looked around and saw the light had almost been painted over with darkness. They needed to find their way out now. He was so tired he could hardly recall the reason he had come into the forest in the first place, and he desperately needed sleep. It seemed as though he hadn't slept in days.

His grip on the girl's hand slackened, and she squeezed tighter, pulling him onto another path. "I've got it now."

Vince's head felt fuzzy. His body ached. It took him a moment to register what was happening. "You've got what now, sweetheart?"

"The path home. I know where we are. We'll be home soon, silly." She smiled up at him. He smiled back.

Her questions started up again.

"Are you married?"

"I was."

"What was her name?"

"Jane."

"That's a good name. Why aren't you married anymore?"

"I don't know. Can we talk about something else, honey?"

The girl stopped again and looked up at Vince with a sly smile. "You forgot my name, didn't you?"

Vince tried to play it off, sifting through the memories in his head, trying to remember what she had said. It felt like their conversation about names had been days ago. They had to have been walking for hours and hours at this point, but when he looked around there was still a bit of light clinging to the forest floor. "I'm sorry. I don't know why I can't remember your name."

The girl shrugged. "It's Brittany, silly." Brittany pulled on his arm to bring him closer. "It's okay though. I can't remember your name either."

"It's—" he had to think for a moment. He figured he was absolutely exhausted if he couldn't remember his own name. His brow furrowed and it came to him. "It's Vince. You can call me Vince. You don't have to call me Detective anymore." He didn't remember telling her he was a detective. But he must have early on in their expedition.

"Okay, Vince." And with that she pulled on his arm leading him to another path.

They walked along in silence for a long time, allowing Vince to think about the situation. He remembered getting lost in the woods because he had been looking for something. He didn't have a dog, or any pet, so he knew it wasn't that. Had he been out here looking for this girl? Her parents must have called the precinct saying she had gone missing, and now he had found her, and he was getting her back home. He distinctly remembered her saying she wanted to get home.

Taking a risk, he said aloud, "I'm glad I found you. Your parents are worried sick about you."

She smiled up at him and said, "I know. It was an accident. But I'm pretty sure they stopped looking for me a long time ago."

A twinge of compassion hit his heart and he replied, "Oh honey, I'm sure they haven't given up on you. It hasn't been that long. And you're with me now, and we are getting out of this forest. You and me together."

A glimmer of hope in her eyes was followed by a wave of sadness and she continued to walk in silence.

He looked around and noticed that moonlight was filtering through the trees, and he wondered how late it was, and what exactly he was doing out in the forest in the middle of the night. Feeling the hand holding his he looked down at the little girl and asked, "Honey, do you know where we're going?"

The girl let out a surprisingly adult bitter laugh and said, "You forgot my name again."

He felt hurt at the accusation, but as he tried to recall her name, he found he couldn't. Resigned to the embarrassment, he sighed and said, "You're right. I have forgotten your name."

He hadn't only forgotten her name; he had forgotten why they were out here. Taking a few deep breaths to focus his mind he felt his body aching beneath the weight of their excursion.

The girl said, "It's Brittany. I think I remember your name, but could you tell me one more time? I won't forget this time."

He frowned, wondering at how difficult it was to keep anything in his head. Maybe he had a concussion. Had he fallen? He moved his free hand over his head, looking for any wounds or bumps, but found none. "Ummm..." was all he could manage at first. His eyes closed and he was afraid they wouldn't open again, but when they did, he found the little girl staring at him intently. "Did you ask me a question?"

She giggled and shook her head. "No. We're almost there."

As she began to tug on his arm, he stood still, not allowing her to drag him. Nothing made sense. All of the alarm bells inside of him were going off at once. There was something terribly wrong here. Who was this little girl and why were they in the woods? "Almost where?" he asked in a small voice.

She glared up at him with a wolfish grin and replied, "Home."

Once again, she tugged on his arm, and this time he followed willingly. He hoped they would find home soon; he was dog-tired.

4

The two of them stepped up to the edge of a clearing and the man looked around, spying bunches and bunches of mushrooms hedging in the open space.

The girl released his hand and Vincent woke up as if he had been in a trance. He looked down and saw Brittany standing beside him, preparing to enter the clearing ahead of them.

It was full night at this point, but the moon shone brightly into the glade in front of them. Vince kneeled down beside Brittany and put a hand on her shoulder. "Brittany, where are we? This is not the way out of the forest. We need to keep looking for a way out of here." Flustered, he asked again, "Where are we?"

Brittany looked up at him with a large smile on her face and said, "We're home," and stepped into the open space.

Not knowing what else to do, Vince followed her into the clearing. Brittany walked away from him and stepped up onto a stump and held her arms out to her sides.

It was then Vince noticed the other stumps that dotted the clearing. There were six on each side. One by one he watched as girls materialized out of the forest and stepped up onto all the stumps, taking each other's hands until both sides linked up.

Somewhere in the shock response part of Vince's brain he imagined they looked like human lights on a runway. He even uttered a small, frightened laugh. And then he heard the other sound. It began as a low rumble and grew into the sounds of twigs snapping and logs creaking. He squinted into the darkness beyond the girls and imagined he saw a set of eyes, glowing softly in the moonlight. The girls at the far end held their free hands out and it appeared to Vince as though branches reached out and grasped them firmly.

All of the girls pivoted their heads to look at Vince. The two girls closest to him spoke, "Take our hands," and held out their free hands toward him.

Instinctively, he took a step back and reached for his gun. His hand groped for a moment before his brain filled in the gap: his holster and gun were missing. He distinctly remembered bringing them with him, but where could they have gone?

The girls smiled politely at Vince. "Please take our hands. If you do not, we will kill you." The words came out of different mouths, disorienting him. He didn't know where to look. By the time he turned to the speaker another of them was talking, finishing the sentence, beginning a new one. It was as if they were all interconnected. With whatever was hiding in the shadows at the far end of the clearing.

Reluctantly, Vince stepped forward and held his shaky hands in front of his body. It felt like his arms were alien creatures that had attached themselves to his body in place of his actual appendages. They moved on their own, and he was both terrified and madly curious to discover what would happen when he made contact.

Before he could have second thoughts and retract his arms, the girls reached out and grasped his hands firmly. A jolt of electricity zipped through his body, exiting his mouth in the form of a groan. He squeezed his eyes shut, waiting for the sensation to pass. It didn't leave him entirely, but he could feel himself adapting to the sensation, so he opened his eyes again.

"Very good, Detective Aronson." The voices, all separate, all one.

"What do you want from me?" Vince asked with a bit more fear in his voice than he wanted to convey.

"You have been searching for me. I have made myself known." The effect of the many voices was spine-chilling. Vince tried to slough off the feeling.

"You are the Wendigo then." It was a statement.

"I have gone by many names, even before the first indigenous peoples arrived. I have existed for many millennia."

"But I would know you by Wendigo, yes?" A wave of vertigo passed over Vince.

"Yes."

"I've been looking for you because people from my town are dying. And it has been said that you're the cause of this."

A dry chuckle came from the darkness. It sounded like dried leaves crunching under a bootheel. "I am the effect of this. I caused nothing. Where greed exists, I am necessary. You destroy the lands and each other, believing there will be no consequences. Yet the ripples never cease. They expand beyond space and time. The impact is felt for lifetimes."

"You're saying we caused you to exist? How?"

"Your inquisitive nature is why you will be a valuable asset among us. I do not seek out to destroy, but I must feed, or I shall perish. And this generation is ripe to pick."

"So, you would wipe out all of us?"

"Aside from those who stand by my side. I could feed for multiple ages on all the lifeless souls in existence at this point in the linear."

"And if I refuse to assist you, I will perish with the rest." It was more of a statement than a question, but the Wendigo answered by sending an excruciating pain through Vince's entire body. He almost crumpled to the ground, but the feeling released before it overpowered him fully.

"You are not nutrient rich. You would be but a morsel, a scrap of meat left on the bone for me to suck at."

"So, you'd rather make me one of your own, instead of wasting me as fuel."

A ripple passed through the girls, and he felt the affirmative in his body rather than audibly.

"I would like to show you something, Detective. I would like to open your consciousness to the infinite of the universe. You will understand all you need to make your decision once you have seen."

"The infinite of the universe? Like the past, present and future?"

Another shudder. "Time does not lie down straight like bricks on a path. Time does not obey your archaic concepts of linear motion."

Vince had read about the concept of time existing all at once, that it was multi-dimensional as opposed to flat. "You mean everything exists right now? Right here?"

A smile grew on each face Vince could see, and it filled him with a cold dread. He shivered, watching the echoes of the movement trace all the way back to the darkness where he heard the slight shaking of the indistinct creature he could not see.

"That is a rudimentary explanation, but hints at an appropriate concept."

A new thought occurred to Vince. "Why are you showing up now? Why wait for however long you waited to appear at this particular time?"

"My bonds have been removed. I am gaining my strength and I shall escape my prison once and for all."

"What bonds?"

"The cairns of stone that surrounded my resting place have been taken away."

Vince remembered the conversations with George and Sara, attempting to shield his mind from the probing he felt. He believed that the Wendigo could see his skepticism, and that is why he hadn't killed him already. Vince held onto that line of thought, hoping it shone through enough to confound the creature.

"And you have no holy men left to properly bind me to this place. Superstition has become demonized, so beliefs are now transactional. Imagination is unholy with regards to spiritual awakenings."

Good, let this thing believe that, Vince thought to himself. Aloud he said, "And yet you remain here, unmoving."

"I have not the strength yet to fully return. My binds may have been broken, but I am weak. This is why I recruit. My disciples are extensions of my being. I will bring them to you once you have agreed. You will be of one mind with me and those who are faithful."

"Like these girls. Are they disciples?" Vince could feel anger rising in his chest, but he tried to keep himself calm.

"These are necessities. Nothing more. I will have no need for them once I have regained full strength."

"And what happens to them when you no longer need them?" Vince was finding it difficult to remain passive in his questioning, but he had never been trained to stay calm when talking to an ancient creature of myth, so he cut himself a little slack.

"They will return to the earth as dust. Return to the universe from whence they came."

A thought crossed Vince's mind and he blurted it out, "How are they able to leave if you are unable?"

"They are extensions of me. They do not lack the strength as I do."

"Why don't they return to their homes? Why do they stay?"

"They believe in me. They believe in my purpose. And many of these vessels have been with me for centuries. Their home is here."

Vince felt compassion for the girls, and an intense hatred for the Wendigo. This creature calmly separated children from their parents and spoke of them as if they were inanimate objects.

"We run low on time. You must make your decision." This time all the girls spoke in unison.

Vince thought about it for a moment and then, with a smile said, "You told me all time exists always. It's past, present, future stacked on top of each other."

"It is that way for me. But you do not believe it, so it does not exist that way for you."

Vince involuntarily tried to take a step back, but the grip on his hands held firm. "That's not how the world works. We don't simply get to believe up our own rules. People have tried to do that since the beginning of time, and it never turns out well."

"Belief is an enormously powerful tool in shaping the universe. Individually, your belief may alter your perception of reality. Collectively, belief can alter the fabric of the physical world."

Vince's head reeled as he thought of the implications of the Wendigo's statement. "But facts are facts. Laws are laws. Gravity holds me to this planet. Oxygen allows me to breathe. These are inescapable truths."

"Because that is what you believe. Do you have enough faith to believe something other? Doubt fills every aspect of humanity. With pure faith and belief, the *rules* you hold so dear are able to be rewritten."

"That's not true." Vince couldn't fully process all that was being said. There were too many paradoxes in logic, too many caveats. "If the rules can be rewritten, and if belief and faith can alter the reality of our existence, why can you not escape this place?"

"Belief can be transferred to relics. They are a vessel. Ordinary objects become imbued with the power of the mind and soul. If the belief is strong enough those relics become impenetrable."

Frustration rose in Vince, and he decided to ask a cheeky question. "There are people who believe with all their hearts that the earth is flat. It's been proven otherwise. How do you explain that?"

"Pure, unflinching faith puts blinders over the eyes of the being, allowing them to perceive reality differently than others."

"But only for them?"

"The more collective the belief, the stronger the reality shift. Enough pure, unwavering agreement and the physical nature of the universe alters from the smallest cell upward. This is why seeds of doubt are important. Individuality is essential. Without those pieces of wonderment, the world as you know it would cease to exist."

"The earth would disappear?"

A shudder of anger passed through the girls, hitting Vince like a wave of sound. "You do not listen. It would not exist as you know it. It would alter; shift."

"Everyone believing the same thing is dangerous?"

"It is for a species that harbors such selfish desires and hatred in their hearts. If you were to realize the potential available if you all worked together you would destroy yourselves. There is not enough benevolence within you as a whole to repair any damage that would be done.

"There was a place, thousands of years ago, in a region called Babylon where the collective of humanity attempted to work together to reach God. This bridge existed before doubt and was holy and pure. But when the first humans gained the knowledge of good and evil it severed the sacred connection to the creator.

"The attempt to reconnect with your God presented a problem. This entity knew that to restore a direct connection would be to destroy their creation. And the relationship that had been built out of the fractured whole was one of free will. The ability to decide your own way through life. Your God did not want slaves. They wanted you.

"The creator confused you enough to make it impossible to build your way to extinction. The altering of tongues planted the seeds of doubt necessary to save the creation."

Vince's head hurt and he closed his eyes. There was no way any of this was real. He remembered the patches of mushrooms as he passed into the clearing and determined that he must be in the throes of hallucination again. He opened his eyes and said, "You believe in God?"

"In this dimension, yes. I believe in the God who created this universe."

"Are you an inter-dimensional being then?"

"I exist in many dimensions simultaneously. This one is one of the more powerful existences. It is rich with the nutrition I need to exist."

"I don't understand."

"Then allow me to show you." All the girls in unison once again.

Vince felt as though he were about to hyperventilate, but he nodded his head and replied, "Okay."

The sound of a hundred trees rustling rose up in the shadows, and Vince found himself looking up and up until he could just make out the indistinct features of the Wendigo. It moved toward him out of the shadows, and he got his first real look at the creature and had to stifle a scream.

The face was that of a skeleton, with sunken eyes that swiveled in their sockets. They were black in black. It appeared that vines and trees had woven their way between the spaces and had become one with the being. The nose and mouth protruded slightly, giving the impression of something not quite human, yet not exactly Cervine.

Rising from the Wendigo's head was a giant set of antlers that looked sharp enough to skewer him where he stood. There were cracks and fissures within the winding horns.

Flesh hung loose and sparse from the torso of the creature, exposing tree-like ribs as they shifted and swung. The arms were gaunt and ended in bony hands that were eerily human.

Completing the abomination in front of him were its legs that ended in powerful hooves. The knee joint bent backwards like an elk, which gave it an unnatural movement that almost loosened Vince's bowels.

At its full height it stood nearly as tall as the trees around it, and in three hulking steps it stood before Vince. Leaning down it looked Vince directly in the eyes and Vince could smell the rot wafting from it. The Wendigo snorted, inciting a wave of nausea within Vince.

For a moment, the man and the creature regarded each other silently. The eyes of the Wendigo creaked as they swiveled in their sockets. Vince didn't dare blink while confronted by this being. He could feel the Wendigo searching his mind, invading his privacy. It was a grievous and uncomfortable violation, and for a split-second Vince thought he saw the history of this creature played out all at once.

Then the Wendigo reached out and touched Vince's forehead with the tip of its finger. Everything exploded in Vince's head and then went quiet.

YOUNG

SEPTEMBER 20

YOUNG

1

Vince's head pounded, the pain and pressure nearly unbearable. He groaned and clenched his teeth and felt something gritty between them. He felt something crunch and then someone was standing over him. He couldn't make out what they were saying, but it seemed to be directed toward him.

A hand grabbed his face and another hand attempted to pry open his mouth. He fought it, slowly returning to consciousness. Fingers groped in his mouth, and he nearly bit down on them before the owner extracted them.

His head reeled, an intense feeling of something wriggling through the canyons of his brain.

The voice was slowly clearing up, but it still felt garbled in his head. Maybe they were speaking another language. Then there was a sharp sting on his cheek, which woke him up to near full cognizance. He groaned, eliciting a response from the other person with him.

"Finally!" the voice exclaimed. Vince couldn't determine if they were angry or elated.

He dared a peek through his eyelashes and saw a blurry figure above him, holding something. The figure came closer to his face with the something and a sharp odor infiltrated his nostrils, causing him to sit bolt upright. His eyes flung open, and his vision cleared. He looked around and saw Lew standing in front of him.

"Sweet damn, it's about time you woke up." He looked a bit bemused, but also slightly angry.

"Where am I?" Vince looked around taking in his surroundings, but everything in his head hurt and it was difficult to focus.

"I found you in the woods, taking a nap with a beautiful bunch of mushrooms. You found a whole field of them. You're lucky I was the one that found you. If anyone else would have gone out into the woods you'd be in a room, padding and all. Instead, I brought you back to your shed." The sense of immediacy slowly dissipated from Lew's tone.

"In the woods?" His brain felt like a lock and the key wasn't fitting quite right; the tumblers weren't falling.

"You went out to the woods to find the Wendigo or whatever fairy tale and then you stopped answering your phone. Your GPS looked like someone who had lost his keys. Then your phone must've died because I lost the trail. I got nervous and went looking for you. Took nearly the entire night to find you." Lew sounded hurt.

"I'm sorry. I think I remember wandering the woods, but most of it is a blur after that. I'm trying to piece it together, but most of the pictures are missing." Vince shook his head to try and jog his memory.

"At least we know why Martin was eating all those bunnies and rodents."

Vince furrowed his brow, not understanding.

"The mushrooms have some sort of effect that makes you hungry. Starving. Luckily, I found you when you were on your appetizer, so I figured it was safe to not take you to the hospital and get your stomach pumped."

As Lew spoke, Vince's mind stutter-stepped its way to a knowledge of what he was saying, and he instinctively began spitting. That's what the crunch was, the grit between his teeth. "Oh God," he moaned quietly.

Lew continued as if Vince was sitting still and listening to every word he said. "I charged your phone and the tox report came back from the lab. They say the level of psychotropic elements is off the charts. Even inhaling a few spores could cause hallucinations and I found you rolling around in a grove of them. You got a quick email from that expert you sent the samples to, and he said he had never seen levels or variations of psychotropic elements within a single type of mushroom. He believes a few varieties of mushrooms have been crossbreeding, creating a new species. All in all, he sounded very excited about the find."

Vince felt himself returning and joined the logical train of thought, ignoring the bit about the expert and his scientific discovery. "No wonder I don't remember anything. I'm sure I will at some point, but for now I need water. I need to hydrate."

Lew handed a bottle of water to Vince, and he drained it neatly.

"Could you find the place where you found me if you needed to?"

A look of concern from Lew. "You can't be serious."

Vince held out his hands. "I'm not saying I want to go back out there, but if I needed could you get me there?"

Lew bit his lip, thinking. Then he shook his head. "Doubtful. I was more concerned with getting you out of there than anything else. The GPS tracking was the only thing that kept me from getting lost."

Vince nodded his head slowly, still feeling his awareness floating freely a bit. He looked outside and saw it was dark. "Morning or evening?"

"Morning," came the reply.

"That's good."

Lew looked at Vince. "Why is that good?"

Vince lowered his head, feeling like he had to do something, and quickly, but it eluded him. "I don't know."

Testing his legs, Vince walked to the table in the middle of the room. There was an essential piece missing from this whole situation, but it kept slipping behind doors in his head. He was out in the woods looking for the Wendigo. Instead of the Wendigo he had found a field of mushrooms. But what happened in the middle? Why couldn't he remember anything between stepping into the forest and waking up here?

He banged his hand on the table, which sent a jolt of pain up his arm. As he rubbed his arm, he kept asking himself what he couldn't remember. There was something right there, dancing at the edge of his memory. Something about...a girl? Was there a girl in the woods?

In a flash it all came back to him. There *was* a girl. She was lost. And they couldn't find their way out. But then she had led him to a clearing. And there were more girls.

Lew watched the expression change on Vince's face and moved in closer. "What is it, Vince?"

Vince looked up and told Lew everything he remembered. There were bits and pieces missing in the middle, but it all ended face-to-face with the Wendigo. By the time he had finished he was out of breath and sat heavily into a chair.

Lew thought about it for a long while before responding, "So you are saying the Wendigo is really out there? Is that what you want me to believe?"

"I can see it clear as day in my head. It looked like a tree come to life. And all the girls were connected to it; girls from all walks of life and all times enslaved by this thing. They spoke for it. Or..." He struggled with describing it properly, "he spoke through them."

Lew released a dry laugh between his lips. "That is one hell of a hallucination, partner."

Vince stopped and thought about it. He wasn't certain it had been a hallucination. But was there any way to be convinced it wasn't? He had no idea how to approach the information. "I mean, I guess. But...what if it wasn't a hallucination?"

"If it wasn't then we are all going to be in it deep in the next couple days."

Vince felt himself close to hyperventilating and slowed his breathing, so he didn't pass out. He turned to Lew and asked, "Did Martin do anything weird while I was gone?"

Lew opened his mouth to reply, but before he could, there was a knock on the shed door.

2

Both Vince and Lew turned toward the door. It would have been comical if not for the eerie atmosphere surrounding their conversation. No one outside of that little hut, aside from Vince's ex-wife, had any idea that it even existed, and she had never visited the little outbuilding, not even when they were still together.

Lew made a motion with his eyes, informing Vince there was no way *he* was going to see who was on the other side. Vince wiped his hands on his pants and stepped up to the door. "Can I help you?" He turned slightly to Lew and shrugged.

"Detective, I need to speak with you. It is really quite urgent." The voice was familiar, but neither of them were able to place it. "Detective Aronson, it's Martin. Remember? Martin? The guy who ate those animals?"

Vince turned to Lew quickly and whispered fiercely between his teeth, "What the hell is he doing here?"

Lew had his service pistol in his hand, pointed at the floor, his hand clenching and unclenching the grip. He nodded and Vince turned the knob and slowly opened the door.

Both men sucked air in between their front teeth as they saw Martin, standing in the door frame. It looked as though he hadn't eaten in about a month; he was emaciated. His clothes hung loose, and his cheekbones featured prominently on his face. He was wearing shorts, and the legs poking out of the bottom of them were almost skeletal. His eyes ticked back and forth nervously, and he cocked his head as if he were listening to someone that Vince and Lew couldn't hear.

Vince waved him inside. "What happened to you, Martin?"

Instead of answering, Martin eyed Lew suspiciously. It seemed he was unwilling to speak in front of him.

Vince got his attention again. "Martin, we need to get you to a hospital. What is going on?"

Lew took a step toward Martin and Martin took a step away and raised his hand, pointing a bony finger at Lew. "Not while he's here. He's not one of us. He doesn't belong."

For a moment, Vince was very confused, but then it dawned on him that he might be referring to the Wendigo. But how would Martin be aware of his encounter, especially if it could be chalked up to a bad trip down psychedelic lane? Vince went into detective mode. "Why don't you have a seat? Tell me why Lew doesn't belong. What do you mean by that?"

Martin took the proffered seat and stared deep into Vince's eyes. "You know damn well. He hasn't had an encounter. He hasn't been..." his tongue flicked out of his mouth and licked his lips. It reminded Vince of a lizard. "He hasn't been touched by it."

Lew took a step closer, his pistol still in his hand, barrel to the floor. "If you mean the mushrooms, you're damn right I didn't touch it."

As if Lew had proved a point, Martin gestured to him and raised his eyebrows at Vince. "You see? He doesn't know. He doesn't belong." His focus shifted back to Lew, but he continued to speak to Vince. "He has to leave."

Vince flicked his eyes at his partner; an old signal between them to go along with whatever came next. Vince grabbed another chair and sat down in front of Martin, putting on his sincerest face. "He's okay. I explained everything to him, and he believes. He wants to meet the Wendigo."

A look of awe fell over Martin's features and his mouth dropped open. "He does? How did you convince him?"

"I told him about the girls and their connection to him. How they were in harmony with the Wendigo." Vince tried on a smile, and Martin smiled back.

"And it was so peaceful. It was like being home." A whimsical look entered Martin's eyes and Vince hazarded a glance at his partner.

"And he told me about how we can all change the world if we just work together. We can alter reality." As he spoke, he watched the features on Martin's face shift. It became quickly apparent that he had not been told the same things. He became twitchy once again and pointed an accusatory finger in Vince's face.

"You're lying. You lie. I feel the presence on you, but you speak untruths. You try to put words into the mouth of the Master. I shall cut your tongue out and bring it with me as a sacrifice."

A flash of James hanging on a tree in the forest, his tongue cut out, leapt into Vince's mind. James had blasphemed. He could see Martin getting anxious.

Vince didn't panic, simply switched gears. "I'm not lying, Martin. What I told you was the truth. What were you told? Maybe the Wendigo has a different message for each of his disciples." The word escaped his lips and he immediately felt nauseous at the loaded connotation.

For a moment both Vince and Lew were convinced Martin was going to turn on them, but then his features softened, and he nodded his head. "Yes. Yes. That makes sense. Everyone has a different part to play. Everyone needs their own piece of the plan. Of course. That's how we work together as his disciples."

"What piece did the Wendigo give to you, brother?" Vince felt more and more sick, masquerading as a believer, utilizing language of the initiated, but he knew he must continue.

Martin smiled, causing his eyes to sink further into their sockets. He looked hollow. "Did he tell you about time? How time doesn't matter? Because it exists always. Eternity is omnipresent. You can't put a time frame on eternity, because it has no beginning and no end, it simply is." The exaltation in his face intensified as he spoke. Both Vince and Lew knew the signs of fanaticism.

Lew moved closer to the table, pretending to be enraptured by the concepts Martin was expressing. "And once the master returns to full power, this eternity will come into fruition?"

As Martin turned his gaze away from Vince and fixed upon Lew, Vince knew he had accepted Lew as one of them. The blind faith of the overzealous had dulled his gut instincts.

"Yes. Indeed. This is how it shall be. And on that day, we shall have wings to fly. The Master will give us our power and allow us to embrace it as our own."

Martin's eyes had glazed over, and he was caught in the ecstasy of the moment. It allowed Vince and Lew to share a look and then go in to squeeze for any last morsel of information they could gather.

Vince patted Martin on the shoulder and smiled his broadest smile. "The day is fast approaching. Did the master tell you anything else? Give you any instruction on how to finish preparations for his return to power?"

Martin nodded his head fervently. "The Master said that *you* are the one to lead his disciples. You understand more than anyone else and you have the ability to command armies."

This last bit of information shocked Vince, but he realized that this was an opportunity to try and control the situation. "And how many are there of us?"

Martin thought for a moment and then replied, "Nearly two dozen. With your partner here, I would say we land directly on that number."

Vince realized he now had carte blanche, because Martin fully believed he needed to listen to whatever instruction was given him by the leader of the disciples. "And where are the disciples?"

Martin's smile faltered and he cocked his head to the side, puzzled. "Do you not feel them? They are all around. They surround this shed at this very moment."

The revelation sent an all too familiar frozen chill down Vince's back. They were being watched and this could all be a test to see if he were truly one of them. He only had a couple more questions, and then they would all find out if he passed.

"Martin, we don't have much time. I can't find my way back to the master. He has blocked this from me. In order to convert my partner here, I need to know how to get back to the clearing."

Martin shook his head and let out a dry cackle. "You should know, better than any of us, that if someone is truly worthy, they will find their way to the Master. The Master will open the way for them."

A flicker of doubt flashed across Martin's face. Vince stared through the questioning look, hoping his confidence would deflect any further issues.

After a moment, Martin smiled again and said, "I was told by the Master to test you, to ensure you are truly the leader of his disciples." Having said that, Martin brandished a small, curved knife and ran it crossways across his wrist.

Blood poured from the wound, but Martin sat silently, watching Vince intently. The iron smell of the blood hit Vince's nostrils and his vision blurred. Something in the smell aroused a deep hunger within him. That feeling of worms wiggling through his brain. He needed to taste the blood, to tear at the tendons and muscle within Martin's wrist. It was almost too overwhelming to resist. His ability to think clearly was hampered by the desire.

In a faraway region of his brain, Vince knew what he needed to do, but he could feel his revulsion trying to make itself known within the craving. He was also aware he didn't have long to decide before Martin would start to suspect something was wrong.

Out of Vince's periphery he could see Lew moving to get a towel to staunch the flow of blood. Everything moved in slow motion. A moment before Lew reached Martin with a towel and duct tape Vince leapt at Martin and grabbed his arm below the cut. He buried his face into the bloody wrist and sucked at the blood. His teeth found tendons and chomped down on them. He tore at the muscle and tendons, noticing the small jumps Martin's fingers were making, creating a macabre puppet show. Through the gore, Vince could barely make out the horrified expression on his partner's face.

Vince reached gristle and took one last gigantic ripping bite out of Martin's wrist, and he saw the man's hand go limp, useless for the rest of his life. And through the whole ordeal Martin sat silently with a small smile on his face, understanding this test was necessary for the Master to come back to full power. The Wendigo's second-in-command had proven himself by giving in to the greedy desires of the bloodlust.

Finally, Vince wrenched his head away from Martin's arm, his breathing ragged and feral. He was at war within his own mind. One side needed to continue to feast on the flesh of this human, while the other side knew if he didn't stop, he would be lost in the madness that held all these *disciples* in raptured zeal.

He stepped away from Martin and gestured at Lew to bind the wrist, stop the flow of blood. Martin was sheet white and seemed to be losing consciousness. Lew wasn't moving; he was frozen in place by fear and confusion.

Vince moved up and grabbed the towel, wrapping it around Martin's wrist and tying off the ends. He then walked over to a cabinet and pulled out a small acetylene torch, sparking flint in front of the tip to ignite the flame. Then he twisted a knob, and the orange flame became a dagger of blue, angry and bright. Without a thought he whipped the towel off Martin's wrist and applied the flame to the wound, cauterizing it within seconds. Martin let out a silent scream and passed out, his head lolling on his chest.

It was only then that Vince heard the rasping breath in his ear. He turned one way and then another, trying to find the source before he realized that it was his own breath. He knew he needed to calm down, do some damage control before his partner wigged out completely and took off running to the nearest sanitarium or worse, the precinct.

Vince placed the torch on the table, the tip still smoldering with heat, and grabbed Lew by the shoulders. "I had to do it, Lew. We have to stop whatever is going on, and that was a test. I had no choice."

Lew stared blankly through Vince, a string of drool dribbling out of the side of his mouth. Vince was afraid he had lost his partner. There was nothing he could do for him now. In desperation he slapped Lew across the face, hard, and Lew blinked a couple times before staring directly at Vince and screaming. "What in the fuck was that?!"

"If we want to stop this cult, we have to make like we're undercover. I had to do what he wanted me to do, or this would all be for nothing." Vince's breathing had returned to normal, but he could still smell the blood in the air and a piece of him longed to eat again. He knew the words he was telling Lew were the truth, but he was afraid there was a twisted desire underneath that he was trying to pretend didn't exist.

Lew was becoming more cognizant of his surroundings by the

second and he looked at Vince and pointed an accusatory finger in his face. "Your eyes. You wanted to do it. You needed to...eat."

There was nothing Vince could say to convince Lew otherwise, and time was short. He simply nodded his head, his tongue absentmindedly licking at the blood still covering his mouth. "I can't explain it. I don't know how long the effects of the mushrooms remain, but it must last a while. Hopefully, that's the only test I'll have to pass in order for these...people...to trust me."

Lew shrugged, his detective brain kicking in again. "Okay, so what do we do now?"

Vince thought for a moment before snapping his fingers. "We need to tie Martin up and gag him in case any of the interlopers outside decide to become curious. I'll attempt to disperse the crowd, if there even is one, and we can go from there."

Lew put a hand on Vince's shoulder. "We have to take Martin to the hospital. We can't just leave him out here. If anyone were to find out that would be the end of our careers."

Vince shook his head solemnly. "If he wakes up and tells anyone about the little feast that took place that would be the end of my career anyhow. We talked about this. We talked about keeping him here if we needed."

A hesitation from Lew. "We didn't talk about you biting into his arm! Besides, he believes you're the one to lead them when the Wendigo returns to full power. He won't say a word."

"If the mushrooms wear out of his system during his rest and he wakes up aware of himself, who's to say he won't freak out and spill the beans?" Vince was rubbing his forehead furiously with his thumb and index finger. He didn't like any of this, but he couldn't see any other way.

"So, how do we stop these people from proceeding with their

plans?" Lew was still watching Vince intently, waiting for him to lose control again. A rift had been created between them, a chasm that Lew wasn't sure would ever be repaired.

Vince clicked his tongue, trying to come up with a plan. When he moved quickly toward the door, Lew flinched, his hand instinctively moving toward his waist. If Vince noticed, he didn't say anything. "Tie him up and I'll take care of our crowd of witnesses outside. We'll go from there."

Lew nodded and moved to get a rag and some rope.

Vince opened the door and the soft light of the early morning peered through, pinpointing all the dust motes hanging in the air.

Looking around, Vince caught a glimpse of at least ten people watching from the woods. They were all in various stages of starvation. None were as far gone as Martin, but he could see the sharp cheekbones on most.

He cleared his throat and yelled out, "Martin has administered my test and I have passed. You can see from the blood around my mouth." A whispered awe swept through the onlookers. "He is now resting and is not to be disturbed until after the master's ascension. He has done his part."

Vince paused, making sure he was the absolute center of attention. This was the tricky bit. He might be able to stop them if they genuinely believed he was their leader.

"I have spoken to the master. He has informed me that he is in no need for any more human sacrifices. When the Autumnal Equinox arrives the day after tomorrow, he will rise up and take over, but until that time we are to prepare by meditating. We must send all of our energy toward the master to help strengthen him."

As he spoke, Vince inwardly winced. The words sounded ridiculous coming out of his mouth, and if even one of them didn't believe him they would turn on him. He watched as they looked one to another, trying to determine if this was truly how it was to be.

After nearly a minute a woman took two steps out of the woods, a spokesperson. "We will await the Master and prepare as he has requested. The Autumnal Equinox is nearly upon us and then we shall see victory and dominion over all the earth."

There was an awkward silence. Vince realized they were waiting for him to speak again. He didn't know what to say, so he threw out the only thing that made any sense, "For the master."

The chorus of *For the Master* that hit his ears made it seem as though there were hundreds of them out in the forest, but he hoped fervently that it was limited to the ten he could see.

He turned to go back inside the shack, and he heard the disciples shuffling away silently. He prayed they would listen to his words and not hurt anyone else.

3

After making certain that Martin was bound and gagged properly in the shack, Vince informed Lew he had a few errands to run to try and make more sense of the situation. Lew was at a loss as to what his role in the whole thing was, so he decided to patrol the edge of the forest, to make sure no one from the cult decided to make a move.

Vince went into his house and showered for nearly half an hour, scrubbing at his skin, making sure no bloodstains remained. He brushed his teeth multiple times trying to get the taste of blood out of his mouth. It didn't work. Then he took the clothes he had been wearing and shoved them in a burn barrel behind his house and incinerated them.

His first stop was going to be his ex-wife's office. He needed to get a little more information and he hoped she could help him formulate a plan of attack. In his decades as a detective, he had never felt so lost during a case. He had yet to make a single arrest, had bitten into a guy's arm, had hallucinated because of a bunch of mushrooms, and had seemingly encountered a mythological being known as the Wendigo.

Then there was the distance he felt open up between him and Lew. He wasn't sure they would be able to work together after this. Whatever had happened felt irreparable. They would never again be in sync the way they always were in the past. That was the saddest piece for Vince. He didn't have many people that he held close, but Lew was one of them.

He stared ruefully into the barrel as his clothes burned and tears sprung to his eyes. He didn't understand what was happening, but he refused to believe this Wendigo creature was a reality. The brain did funny things, and hallucinations could seem as real as the person sitting next to you. That was all this was. Vince was sure of it.

4

Vince entered Jane's office. There was no sound of a metronome, and for some reason that put him on edge more than the actual ticking sound. Maybe it was simply the tensity of the last week-and-a-half finally catching up to him. Or perhaps Jane had known he was coming and wanted to keep him off balance. She had a way of doing stuff like that to gain her upper hand.

Jane sat behind her desk, typing away at some report or other and it took her a good minute to move her fingers away from the keyboard and look up to acknowledge Vince's presence in the room.

"Back again I see. Still having problems?"

Vince nodded.

"You back to discuss the mushrooms again?"

"In a way."

He relayed everything that had happened, conveniently leaving out the part where he had chowed down on some poor guy's arm and ingested some of him.

Jane frowned through most of the tale, and then she inhaled deeply and exhaled through her nose, the slightest whistling sound escaping her nasal passages.

"You look thinner, Vincent. Have you been taking care of yourself?"

Vince shrugged. "As best I can, considering the circumstances.

Jane nodded. "And how about the drinking? You still nursing that old habit?"

Vince was about to confirm her suspicions when he stopped himself. He couldn't remember having a single drink since...the night he had his first hallucinogenic experience. "Actually, I don't think I've touched a drop in nearly a week. Maybe I've been too busy trying to solve this case."

"Perhaps. It is possible your brain has been so preoccupied that it hasn't had a chance to process a desire for alcohol. For your health's sake I hope that appetite doesn't return to you after this is all wrapped up."

Vince found himself hoping that as well. He even tried to think of his favorite Scotch and the feel of the burn as it slid down his throat, but there was nothing there. He didn't want a drink. He wanted…something different. Unbidden, his mind turned to the blood gushing out of Martin's arm that morning. He felt his salivary glands release, filling his mouth. A slight metallic tang accompanied the liquid. He looked at Jane and for a brief moment he didn't see his ex-wife. Instead, he saw a being ready to be consumed; a feast laid out before him. He blinked the image away, Jane watching him intently.

"What happened right there?" Jane asked, the tone of the therapist coming through loud and clear.

Vince shook his head a bit and then smiled. "Nothing. I really can't remember having a craving over the last few days and I'm a little shocked by that."

"Again, that's not necessarily a bad thing. Be cautious not to replace one vice with another. That can be just as dangerous if it's destructive in nature."

Jane stared intently at Vince, knowing he was hiding something, but recognizing the fact that if she tried to push, he would disappear, hiding his secret forever. "Why did you come to see me today?"

"I wanted to ask you about group psychosis. The last time I was here you told me about the Wendigo syndrome, and I believe that this cult we're dealing with might be suffering from some variation of the disease. Is that possible?"

Vince crossed his fingers, hoping it wouldn't be the case. Hoping that mob mentality had taken the group of people who had been hovering around his house early this morning.

"If it's communicable in some way, it is possible. There might even be something in the mushrooms that alters the brain chemistry and brings about the psychosis. That seems like the most logical explanation, actually."

Jane had furrowed her brow, one of her eyebrows moving up and down as she thought, reminding Vince of one of the idiosyncrasies that had brought about his falling in love with her.

She continued, "If each of them has come into contact with those mushrooms…" her voice trailed off and she looked up at Vince. "You came in contact with those mushrooms."

Vince shifted uncomfortably and nodded his head once.

"Do you have any of these tendencies?" Jane asked cautiously.

"What tendencies?" Vince knew what she was asking but didn't want to admit it to himself.

A fire lit in Jane's eyes. The protective look she tended to assume whenever she was frightened for someone she cared about. "You know what tendencies."

There was a long, tense silence between them and then Vince finally broke it. "I find the idea of human flesh alluring. Yes."

Jane looked away from him, but not before he saw the fear in her eyes. He really wanted to end the conversation there, but she needed to know about his last hallucination. "There's more," he said in a small voice.

Jane returned her gaze to Vince, and he could see tears brimming in her eyes. Up until that moment Vince hadn't feared what was happening. But seeing Jane sitting in front of him tearing up broke him apart. He trusted her with her diagnoses, something she had always figured out with the utmost clinical professionalism. So, to have her shaken badly by the news of someone she used to love intimately admitting to cannibalistic tendencies was unnerving, to say the least.

"During my last hallucination I imagined I spoke to the Wendigo. I had a conversation with him."

"The last hallucination? How many times have you hallucinated, Vincent?" The motherly tone she employed when she was tense came soaring through the words.

"Only twice. The second time was when I was trying to find any hint of the Wendigo, based on witness testimony of having spoken to him."

He raised his hands and shrugged his shoulders. It was what it was.

Jane asked Vince what happened during the conversation and Vince gave her the whole rundown ending with him taking a bite out of Martin's arm.

During the story Jane's face remained stoic, but Vince could see the fear and sorrow deepen in her eyes.

"I see," was all she could muster at the conclusion of the tale.

"So, I'm trying to figure this out. How long the desire will last, if it's permanent, anything."

"You need to have your brain scanned. I know people who do that sort of work. They'll be able to tell you if something has been altered."

Her voice had returned to neutral, and she shuffled papers around on her desk. This was the other side of the coin that Vince knew all too well. When Jane started shuffling papers it meant the conversation was ending and nothing anyone said could change that.

"I only have two days before I think something big is going to happen. They talk about it as The Wendigo gaining enough strength to leave its place of imprisonment due to the Autumnal Equinox. I have to see this through until then. After that I will get checked. I promise."

Vince made a move toward her, but she looked up at him and it was apparent he had become the patient and she was the doctor. There was no personal connection anymore. It was time for him to leave.

"Very well. I will call my people and let them know you'll be contacting them in the next few days. I wish you all the luck with your investigation and I hope we can chat again after its conclusion."

And that was it. The end. Anything Vince said after that point would be returned to him with cool indifference in an attempt to make him leave quicker.

"Thank you, doctor," was all he managed as he walked out the door, heading toward his second stop of the day; one he never thought in a million years he would be making in his lifetime.

5

Vince couldn't believe how quickly the day had gotten away from him as he entered the church. The sun was already casting long shadows and the autumn air cooled the atmosphere dramatically in a matter of minutes.

He walked through the lobby and opened the doors to the nave. Slowly walking between the lines of pews he saw an altar boy snuffing out candles and could faintly hear organ music being piped through the hidden sound system. He reached the third row and slid onto the pew, leaning against the one in front of him, hands crossed. His eyes slowly closed as he listened to the organ playing hymn after hymn.

Vince took a deep breath and opened his eyes. Up in the sanctuary was a pulpit, baptismal font, and a giant cross with Jesus mercilessly crucified upon it. A priest was checking the backs of pews for communication cards and saw Vince sitting alone. He surreptitiously angled toward Vince and sat down in the pew in front of him.

"I don't believe I've had the pleasure of meeting you before, son." The priest had a melodic voice, his face kind and warm.

Vince shook his head. "I haven't been in a church in a very long time." The priest remained silent for a long while, prompting Vince to add, "Kind of was spoiled on the whole idea when I was a kid."

The priest nodded his head and offered him another smile. "I can certainly understand that. It tends to happen when the religious institution molds God into their own image."

Vince thought about that for a moment and then nodded.

The priest continued. "Something tells me you're not here to join our choir or become a member of the church. Do you have a confession to make?"

"No, nothing of that sort," Vince replied. "It's more of a theological inquiry. Something I heard and wanted to confirm or dispel."

"All right. Hit me."

"I was speaking to…" Vince paused for a moment, realizing if he told the priest he had been speaking to some mythological being he might not be taken quite so seriously. "…a friend about the Tower of Babel. He told me that the reason God didn't allow it to become a bridge to heaven was because if humanity connected that directly to the source they would be destroyed. And God didn't want that, because He created us to be in relationship with Him with personal agency. So, God jumbled up the languages and made it impossible for the people to finish the connection."

The priest frowned. "That's an interesting take, but may I make a suggestion?"

Vince made a gesture inviting him to proceed.

"People like to think of the Bible as either all literal or all allegorical. Learning to read the texts within the right context can help decipher reality from parables, if you will. Morality stories. The shepherd leaving the 99 sheep to find the one. The prodigal son. Those are stories meant to teach."

The priest paused and looked at Vince, asking without asking if he was following. Vince nodded once and the priest continued. "So, when we look at the idea of the Tower of Babel, we have to look at it as more of a metaphor. Mankind is constantly attempting to separate from their own humanity. Look at our literature, our superhero tales, our mythologies. We want to rise to the heights of the gods. We are not content in our own humanness. Instead of coming together to assist each other where we are, we try to separate and reach the heights alone and then take power as we imagine that our projections of God do.

"God meets us in our illusions of separation and the brokenness of our souls in order to meet us where we are. We were created to be in relationship, and the idea that God would confuse us out of relationship and towards power and separation doesn't make a whole lot of sense. We become the architects of our own demise. We set the standards for miscommunication, because we want things to be our way, to go the way that benefits us most.

"It sounds to me like this friend of yours is using a technique to make it sound like we have holy intentions in our endeavors, but if you look beneath the surface, they are really saying that separation is the only way. In order to see God, we must separate from God. If we want a relationship with God, we must leave a certain amount of distance, which takes out the idea of intimacy, which is a key component in relationship." The priest chuckled. "Is any of this making sense?"

Vince rubbed his chin and slowly nodded. "Yeah. I think so. The story of the Tower of Babel is to show us the futility of trying to become gods, because we were not made that way."

"And our delusion separation after the garden of Eden means we need a conduit, or better, a revelation of reality, which is the true Word of God, God who fully joins us in our humanity, Jesus."

Vince glanced up at the cross depicting the crucifixion. "My friend is trying to make it seem like we have to become godlike in order to truly reach God, and God wants to keep us at arm's length."

"Seems that way."

Vince released a forced laugh between his teeth. "That's a hell of a thing."

The priest smiled. "Truly a Hell of a thing."

"I appreciate your time, Father. I never thought I would find myself in a church ever again, but I think you actually helped me out today." Vince stood and shook the priest's hand.

The priest stood and clapped Vince on the shoulder. "If you ever have any more questions, or you are curious about God, and even if you're not, you're always welcome here."

Vince turned to leave but stopped and turned back. "One last question. My friend believes that humanity as a whole is greedy and selfish and only out for the individual's best interests. Do you think that's true?"

The priest thought for a long moment before responding, "I believe there are many individuals who are in it for themselves, but I would invite you to pay attention the next time a tragedy occurs. Look for the heroes. They are always there. I happen to have a high view of humanity, which some people call naivete. I would rather believe the best in people than expect the worst.

"You can also look to your deepest longings, below the struggle for power and self-centered importance. I believe you will find there the longings to be authentic and good and truthful and kind. Those are deeper and therefore truer than our surface brokenness."

The two men looked at each other and then Vince nodded and exited the church. As he did, a tear slid down one cheek. Why, he didn't know. He wiped it away and glanced at his watch, realizing it was time to meet up with Lew at the diner and run through their notes and plan out the next day. The last day before whatever was going to happen would happen.

6

Vince's drive over to the diner put him on edge. He had lived in this place for so many years he had become accustomed to the feel of it. But this evening, as he passed by all the businesses that occupied Main Street, they had an ominous, even sinister weight to them.

The feed store, that used to give kittens away for free now had multiple windows boarded up from vandals, the small cinema that played art films and had been the location of Vince's first dates throughout the years, only had a few letters dotting the marquee, and not enough to decipher what was playing there. The burger shop that was really the only competition to the diner had a sign on the door indicating it was closed temporarily. Everything made him feel like a stranger in his own town.

Even the diner had letters out on the neon sign, and it felt as though the light didn't carry as it once had through the doors, and the moment Vince stepped inside he knew something was awry. The place went silent, and everyone looked his direction. Some even had the decency to clock him out of the corner of their eyes. A few gave him knowing nods, as if he shared a secret with them. Even Lauren stood with a freshly brewed pot of coffee clutched in her right hand, staring at him.

It felt as though the air had been sucked out of the room and he felt a heaviness in his chest. He suddenly knew that everyone was aware of what he had been up to, what he had done in the shed behind his house. Everyone was against him, judging him, waiting to call him out on his hypocrisy. His face grew hot, and he wanted to yell at all of them for the accusations they leveled at him without even speaking.

He realized he had been standing in the entryway for a good

minute, but he couldn't make himself move. If he moved, he would do something he would regret. But someone had to pay for the mistrust in the eyes he stared into. Finally, he took one step toward a man with a baseball cap pulled low over his eyes, intending to…he wasn't quite sure, but he would make it known that he was not the one to mess with tonight.

"Over here, ya miscreant," Lew called out from a booth halfway down the restaurant, breaking the spell everyone seemed to be under.

Vince walked toward his partner and slowly the general chatter resumed. He slid into the booth opposite Lew and said, "What was that all about?"

"News travels fast in a small town, mon frere. You know that." Lew had already tucked into a huge plate of bacon, eggs, beans and sausages.

Vince looked at his side of the table and noticed a steak waiting for him. Through a mouthful of food Lew pointed at the plate with his fork and said, "Medium rare. I figured that would do you fine."

Vince tentatively picked up his fork and knife and began delicately sawing at the mostly raw meat. He had never really noticed the sound of cutting steak before, but for some reason it now seemed amplified. It was like listening to tendons snapping, and he could feel the resistance of the sinews of the cheap steak vibrate up through the knife and into his hand. The sensation wasn't completely unpleasant, but it certainly was unnerving. Across from him Lew continued to eat with reckless abandon. Vince figured he hadn't eaten anything all day after witnessing his partner snack on the arm of another human.

"Have you figured out a way we can end all this?" Vince asked, shoving a piece of steak into his mouth and chewing slowly. There was hardly any flavor to the meat. He grabbed the salt and shook it vigorously over the meat.

"Well, considering we have caught zero people in the act of human sacrifice, and we have a person sitting in your shed who only knows what he is supposed to know," Lew began, still chewing a piece of bacon, "I would say we have zilch. We can't mass arrest the people who were standing on your property. I mean, we could arrest them for trespassing, but you dismissed them so quickly we really don't know who any of them are."

Lew took a few large gulps of coffee before continuing. "And seeing as how everything is supposed to happen two days from now there isn't much we can do. I have never felt so useless in my entire life."

His voice was getting louder as he spoke and Vince reached across the table to try and calm him, forgetting the steak knife in his hand. Instinctually, Lew pulled away and the knife sliced through the skin on the back of his hand. Almost immediately blood began welling up through the incision. Vince smelled the blood and leaned forward. He hadn't intended to do such a thing, but the scent was so intoxicating to him, and he suddenly realized how hungry he was.

Lew noticed the slight movement and pushed himself further back into the booth, away from his partner. "Now hold up there, fella. I know you have a penchant for flesh and all, but that doesn't mean you get to gnaw on me."

Vince could tell Lew was trying to keep the situation light, but he also could see the fear in his eyes. There was a part of Lew that thought if given the opportunity, Vince would make him his next meal. The realization saddened Vince, but he could definitely understand the trepidation.

"I'm not going to chew on you, Lew. It was a knee jerk reaction." Vince pointed to Lew's hand. "You'd better wrap that hand up before you bleed all over the place."

Lew reached onto the table and grabbed one of the cloth napkins and spun it around his hand a few times before cinching it tight. "I know, I know. It's just a little weird, yeah?"

Vince feigned shock and replied, "What? Nah. It's just one hell of a mid-life crisis is all."

That got Lew laughing, and he pulled out of his wary state. He returned to his plate of food only to realize he had cleaned it up nicely. He glanced at Vince's nearly untouched steak and raised his eyebrows. Vince pushed the plate across the table. "It's flavorless but have at it."

Lew sawed at the meat and took a giant bite. Spitting bits of steak out of his mouth, he said, "How can you say this is flavorless? You salted it to death. It's nearly jerky at this point."

Vince furrowed his brow and grabbed a small piece of the steak, chewing it thoughtfully. "Nothing. No flavor at all. I might as well be eating silly putty."

"I bet it has to do with those mushrooms. When this is all done, we need to check in with that expert again. I highly doubt anyone has come across hallucinogenic fungus that causes bouts of cannibalism and the inability to taste food," Lew replied.

Vince could tell the mood had shifted, and nothing productive was left in either of them. They both needed a good night sleep and hopefully they would have a fresh perspective come morning.

Wiping his face, although he hadn't really eaten anything, Vince stood up from the table and threw forty bucks down. "I've got this one. Let's reconvene in the morning. If nothing else at least we can support Lauren. How about we say 10am?"

Lew simply nodded and smiled, desperately trying to taste his food through the pillars of salt Vince had placed on top of the meat.

Vince exited the diner feeling frustrated and angry. He had a suspicion that he was about to fail this case. It wasn't a familiar feeling, and he didn't know how to handle it if it came to that. He was afraid that if he didn't solve this before end of business on the 22nd there would be a lot more sacrifices to deal with. And he did not like that notion one bit. So, he turned his car toward home and vowed to get as much sleep as he could before this whole situation came to a head.

7

Vince was in the woods again. He couldn't remember driving to them, but he was standing on a patch of ground surrounded by the mushrooms. Judging by the lack of light it was late at night and the moon was struggling to find a way through the trees.

A twig snapped behind him and he whirled around, not knowing what to expect. But there was nothing there.

He heard breathing behind him, a deep, heavy breath that exuded a sense of calm. He spun again, looking for the source, but like before, nothing.

Then a deep, booming voice rang out: "You have led them astray!"

Vince's right hand scrambled for his gun, but his fingers only found flannel. He was in his pajamas. "Who's there?"

"You are a false follower! You do not believe!" The voice filled Vince's head, rattling his teeth in his skull. It sounded like it came from all around him. No matter where he turned it came from another direction.

"You will be punished for your lack of faith!" Vince continued to spin around, hoping for a glimpse of something to orient himself.

At first there was nothing, but as he inspected the trees, his eyes adjusting to the lack of light, he thought he caught a glimpse of a foot ducking behind a tree trunk.

He focused on the spot for a long while and saw another twitch. His eyes followed the natural growth of what appeared to be a vine, and as his gaze reached the tops of the trees, he could barely make out the silhouette of a creature blending into the foliage.

Vince's heart skipped a beat as he realized what was happening.

The Wendigo was hiding amongst the branches. It was nearly impossible to make it out, but the longer Vince stared, the more subtle movements he caught.

"I see you!" Vince exclaimed.

The Wendigo turned its head and stared directly at Vince. "So, you do!" And it moved toward him with unnatural speed.

Without thinking, Vince turned and ran, hearing the crashing of bushes and ferns as the Wendigo smashed them beneath its weight. Vince took a couple sharp turns, hoping to stay out of the creature's sightline just long enough to gain some ground.

A giant foot stomped the ground two feet in front of Vince, sending him careening in another direction. He felt the wind of an arm swinging through the air, trying to catch hold of him. Panic rose in Vince's throat. He didn't know what to do. The size of the Wendigo made it impossible to escape, but he didn't want to simply give up. Looking to the left and right he could barely make out the faces of the young girls that the Wendigo used as conduits. They were all chanting, "You will pay. You will suffer."

The undergrowth was suddenly thicker, and Vince felt as though he were attempting to run through quicksand. Every step took a monumental effort, and he could sense the Wendigo looming over him. With the last of his strength Vince knelt down and then leapt as high as he could. He felt the Wendigo take a swing and knock him sideways into a tree and he woke up as he thudded to the floor in his bedroom.

His breathing was rapid, and he was on the verge of hyperventilation, but he looked around his room to ensure he was truly there and not still in the forest.

After what felt like twenty minutes, he had calmed his breathing significantly and had convinced himself it had all been a dream.

Nothing to worry about. It was simply a nightmare.

He climbed back into bed, wiping sweat from his forehead and tried to laugh the situation away. But the laugh felt hollow, and Vince fell back asleep, his chest and stomach in knots, fear gripping him tightly.

SEPTEMBER 21

1

Vince stepped into the diner, feeling hungry and exhausted. Thankfully, there had been no more human sacrifices since the one they found a few days prior, which could mean that it was a one and done for the cult, or the followers were simply awaiting instruction from Vince to make another move. The move would have to come soon. Vince felt that if he continued to stall, they would become suspicious and he would most likely become the next victim, tied to a tree with his innards out for the world to behold.

Before he had left for the morning Vince had checked on Martin, who seemed to be in good spirits. He had followed Vince with his eyes, a manic smile on his face, not even attempting to bargain his way out of his binds. Vince had been struck again by the unsettling nature of fanaticism. It put a sharp edge on belief that cut through any normalcy.

As he shut the door to the shed, he had glanced around quickly, hoping to catch one or more of the onlookers from the morning before. Maybe then he could drag one in and try to figure out what exactly was happening in his town. But the woods had been empty, aside from a bunny hopping around, oblivious to the heinous activities of the humans that lived nearby.

Now Vince stood in the entrance to the diner, which was nearly empty save for the few regulars who were there winding down their days from whatever night shift job they worked. Lauren stood behind the bar top counter filling up coffee for Lew who sat on one of the swivel chairs, rocking back and forth ever so slightly.

Vince took a seat next to him, feeling the squeak of the chair as much as he heard it. He clapped Lew on the shoulder, which caused him to jump. Lew's face was haggard, like he hadn't slept a single minute the night before. He looked over at Vince and said, "You look like crap."

"Look who's talking," Vince shot back. "You get any sleep last night?"

Lew scoffed. "I'm worried about you. I know it's only been a few days, but you look like you've lost about 20 pounds."

He grabbed at Vince's clothes, which were indeed sagging off his frame. Vince hadn't even noticed. "And I have zero ideas on what is happening. I wandered the woods all last night, trying to find this field with all the mushrooms. I'm trying to find answers, but there seem to be none. How is that possible?"

Vince watched Lew closely. He knew the signs of obsession, and although Lew kept himself together fairly well, he was developing little tics, which would have been noticed sooner if they had been allowed to work the case together.

He opened his mouth to speak, but Lew interrupted him, "And I feel like I'm losing my train of thought. I can't remember everything. It took me a good five minutes to remember Martin's name. I almost forgot we had him—" his eyes darted around the room, his tongue flicking out of his mouth to provide moisture to his dry lips.

Lew lowered his voice and leaned in close to Vince. "Almost forgot where he was. There's no suspicious activity, no action that would indicate a rising tension before an event. If we hadn't caught Martin and found the body and..." he tried to finish the thought, but Vince just nodded. He didn't need Lew to mention the cannibalistic venture from the day before.

And Lew was right. There was an ominous feeling of something coming, but no evidence to support it. They had nothing to go on, no one to drag in for interrogation. Vince had already played his hand with Martin, attempting to stop any more murders, but he was beginning to suspect no other sacrifices were planned before the big reveal. He had approached this situation all wrong, and now it was spiraling out of control. It was a complete waste of time.

Vince clapped Lew on the shoulder. "Lew, why don't you go get some rest. I'm going to do the same. Tomorrow we can figure out what to do about Martin. He'll keep one more night. And then we will interrogate him properly. Maybe we can get the names of a few others in the cult and scare them enough into becoming a benign entity."

Lew nodded his head. "We should talk to Martin today."

"You're exhausted, and I'm exhausted. I don't think we'd be at the top of our game if we talked to him now." Vince could feel the weight of the last week pushing down on him, gravity increasing so he found it difficult to stand.

"Fair enough," was all Lew could reply.

Lauren walked up and asked if they wanted more coffee. They both refused, but instead of moving on she stood and looked at both of them. After a moment, they both looked up at her and tried to smile.

"You two look like week old garbage," she said.

"So we've been told," Vince whispered.

Lauren set the coffee pot on the counter and leaned down slightly to look them in the eyes. "You been coming in here for years and I don't think I've ever seen you so low. Either of you. Are you working on something we need to be worried about? Should I be visiting some relatives for a while?"

Vince shook his head. "Nothing like that."

He paused, thinking about the past week, and felt like there was nothing harmful in telling her what was going on. There were no suspects. No one to protect, aside from Martin and his whereabouts.

He continued, "We have been looking into a possible cult. They are hurting people and we're trying to stop it. But they have eluded us thus far. We've been chasing the wrong rabbit holes. Sitting here I can think of a dozen more efficient tactics we could have used to end all of this. But I got in my own head. I started to believe the superstitions. And my head hasn't been screwed on particularly tight this whole week. It might be time to retire."

Lauren stood up tall, taking in the information that had just been spewed her direction. Lew was too tired to contribute, so he sat quietly, eyes closed.

"Well, it sounds like one hell of a week, fellas. But you've been behind before. I remember one case you came in frustrated over. Something about music or play lists. You thought you weren't going to catch the guy. Less than a week later he was on trial, and I believe you got him put away for life."

Vince smiled a genuine smile at Lauren. "Thank you, Lauren. I appreciate your kindness. This one feels different though. There's still a piece missing. A gaping hole."

They were all silent for a long time. No one wanted to break the moment. Then the thought of the metronome in Jane's office rose to Vince's mind. The annoying clack of the wand moving back and forth.

He laughed. "I can see Jane's face, her eyebrow raised, asking me if I have a totem to protect myself from the psychosis in my mind."

Lauren suddenly looked more interested. "Totems? Psychosis?"

Vince smiled ruefully. "It seems silly now, but this cult believes that the Wendigo, this ancient mythological creature, will be returning tomorrow on the Autumnal Equinox. There is a syndrome called the Wendigo Syndrome. Jane thinks maybe that is what is happening around here. Some sort of mass psychosis."

Lauren took an involuntary step backward but kept her face perfectly still. "And the totems?"

"I went out to the reservation to get history on The Wendigo and found out that if it was returning to full power that meant whatever was there holding him captive had been removed. But they were speaking metaphorically, of course." He shrugged his shoulders, a sheepish look on his face.

"What sort of thing would be holding him there?" Lauren responded breathlessly.

Vince caught the exasperation and fear in her voice and sat up taller. "Well, they said it could've been totems. Or stacks of rocks called cairns."

"Or decorative stones?" Lauren asked, interrupting Vince's train of thought.

"Perhaps. Why would you say decorative stones?" Vince felt that now familiar sense of dread start to wind its way around his chest.

"My nephews were talking about some super cool stones they found in the forest last week. They said they found them so deep in the forest they didn't think anyone would mind if they took them." Lauren's cheeks flushed, as if she had taken them herself and was confessing.

Lew sat up, suddenly interested in the conversation again. "Can we talk to the nephews?"

Lauren thought for a moment before answering, "They'll be back in the morning. They went camping with their dad."

"We need to speak to them today," Vince said, a little too forcefully.

"Would that you could, but their dad is super into survivalist techniques and such, so they don't take any cell phones or GPS with them when they go camping. There is literally no way to contact them until they get home." Lauren looked at Vince apologetically.

"Which is tomorrow morning," Vince said.

"Which is tomorrow morning," Lauren replied.

"What time are they getting home?" Vince asked, ripping a piece of paper off the order pad Lauren was holding.

"Usually, they get back from those adventures just before lunch."

Vince tapped the paper and looked at Lauren, "I'm going to need their address and phone number. Do you think the boys would be able to find their way back to the spot where they took the stones?"

Lauren wrote the address and phone number on the paper and slid it back over to Vince. "They've been trained well by their daddy. If anyone can find their way back it would be them. They won't be in any danger, will they?"

Vince shook his head. "No. As soon as we know where the area is we will send them back home. Immediately."

Lauren chuckled nervously. "Why do you want to go back there if you think it's all…metaphorical?"

Vince stood up, throwing a twenty-dollar bill on the counter and grabbing Lew by the lapels of his jacket. "Because if something is going to happen tomorrow, I bet that's where it does. I want to be out there to catch every last son of a bitch before they do any more harm."

"Well, I wish you luck. And be gentle with the boys. They didn't know any better. They were just exploring."

Vince nodded and dragged Lew toward the door without another word. His mind was reeling in a hundred different directions. First things first he was going to need some backup for tomorrow, so he needed to get to the station and talk to the Chief.

Vince and Lew stepped outside, and they squinted in the bright sunlight. Lew staggered off toward his car and Vince let him go. He would talk to him later. Maybe if Lew got some sleep, he would be sharper for the rest of the day and the next one. He was going to need all the help he could get.

2

"What do you mean you can't spare anyone?" Vince felt the anger rising in his throat, setting his face on fire.

The Chief looked across the room at him and shrugged his shoulders. "I have hardly seen you this week and you come waltzing in like we're all waiting anxiously for you to come tell us you needed us. You don't have that kind of power. We have other cases, and everyone is already working overtime."

The Chief's calm tone infuriated Vince. It was as though all the pent-up frustration was being forced to stay hidden inside. Vince felt his face redden and he stuttered for a second before regaining his composure. "I don't know how many people are involved in this. If I go out there undermanned, it might come to shooting."

Vince knew he was laying it on a bit thick, but he didn't know how else to get the Chief to agree with him.

"I don't know what to tell you, Detective. I can't spare the manpower." The Chief picked up a cigar and rolled it between his fingers.

"Then at least give me Lew back. Let me take him with me. Give me some sort of backup." Vince pleaded with the Chief, knowing it was a futile effort.

The Chief thought for a long minute and then set the cigar back on the desk and stood up slowly. "I'll allow Lew to accompany you as a civilian. Anything goes down out there he will be treated as such. I hope I'm making myself clear."

Vince was still riled up and looking for a fight, so he retorted, "Why don't you spell it out for me? Nice, little words so I can fully understand."

221

The Chief took a deep breath. "He will have no rights as a police officer. Anything he does will be scrutinized as a private citizen of the Tri-Cities. He will be on his own."

After a tense few seconds, Vince finally broke down and asked, "What is going on Chief? Why can't you give me any help?"

The Chief took a deep breath. "There have been rumors about a group of people terrorizing neighborhoods, harassing individuals."

"Rumors?" Vince couldn't help his Detective side. He needed more information.

"Every time one of us shows up, there's nothing to see. There's nothing out of the ordinary. A couple people will give descriptions of the people, but there's no likeness in our databases. It's like they're ghosts."

Now Vince could see the tiredness in the Chief's eyes. It seemed to be a contagious effect of the week.

"What are they doing to harass these people?"

The Chief took a deep breath. "Propaganda. Religious. Something about converting to the way of the master or perishing with the other heathens."

At the mention of the master, Vince's jaw clenched. "The master? I think these people are part of the cult I've been hunting down."

"If they are then they are highly organized for a new group. It's like they know when the police will be busy or furthest from the neighborhoods they enter." The Chief rubbed his face with his hand, exasperated.

Vince paced the room, allowing himself to think. These people were going into neighborhoods, harassing people and then disappearing without a trace. He stopped walking and looked at the Chief.

"They're testing the law enforcement system."

"Come again?" the Chief asked, perplexed.

"Yeah, they're testing to see how long the response time is, how much time they have to do their business. It's all to prepare for tomorrow."

"Tomorrow? What's happening tomorrow?"

"The Autumnal Equinox. That is when whatever is going to happen with this cult will happen. They are running tests to ensure success in their mission. This is all connected. We need to figure out their plan and put a stop to it. I need to put a stop to it."

Vince's brain was running at a full sprint, hoping the Chief would recognize the importance of sending officers with him to the forest to capture these cult members in the act.

What the Chief said caused Vince's heart to drop to his stomach.

"I have my officers on full alert, patrolling the streets. They *will* slip up eventually and we *will* catch them."

Vince blinked rapidly. "You mean you still won't send anyone out with me?"

"I don't have the availability. We are stretched thin as it is. They haven't killed anyone yet, so we have to err on the side of innocent but annoying." The Chief sat back in his chair; energy spent.

Vince couldn't believe what he was hearing. "What about James? The body in the forest?"

"Have we linked that to anyone?"

"Not in particular, but it would follow that this cult would be the ones responsible for—"

"Is that good Detective work? Will speculation pass muster in a court? How can we go full tilt at an enigmatic presence that hasn't proven themselves dangerous with a clear conscience?"

"Call it a gut feeling. Doesn't that count for anything?" Vince felt himself losing grip on the situation. He was about to head out to the forest with his partner and a couple kids to try and stop a cult who believed in the Wendigo, and the Chief was giving him no consideration. His head began to spin.

"Gut feelings are inadmissible. They do us no good. I'm sorry, Vincent. The answer is no."

Vince felt the meeting end in the finality of the Chief's last statement. There was nothing else he could say that would change his mind. He was on his own. He shook his head and walked out of the office.

The Chief lit up his cigar and took a couple puffs before exhaling off-white smoke into the air. He looked immensely worried.

3

Vince drove aimlessly, not knowing what to do. His head felt jumbled, like too much information was trying to make its way inside without anything to help filter out the white noise. Every sound made him jump, every flash out of the corner of his eye made him think of the Wendigo.

Without knowing it, Vince found himself sitting outside the forest in the very spot he sat before entering the woods to try and confirm the existence of the Wendigo. It felt as though he were being pulled back in, but he knew if he went in now, he wouldn't return. He would be swallowed up by the trees, never to be heard from again. That would be the end of it.

There was a light tap on his window, but he jumped like an explosion had just gone off. He looked over and saw Lew staring in at him, holding his hands up in apology. Vince opened his door and stepped out of the car.

"Didn't mean to frighten you, partner. I had a feeling you might end up here again. And you haven't been answering your cell phone. This whole thing has got me spooked." Lew shifted uncomfortably from one foot to the other. He was clearly agitated.

Vince took a couple deep breaths before responding, "I'm right there with you. I talked to the Chief today, and he said we will get no help tomorrow. But that you can come along as a civilian."

"Oh, yay. Thanks, Chief." Lew rolled his eyes.

Vince proceeded to tell Lew about his conversation with the Chief earlier in the day. He didn't leave out any of the details, and by the end of the tale Lew was just as livid as Vince had been in the office.

"These are obviously connected. And he's saying we can't do

anything because we're riding by the seat of our guts?"

Vince nodded. "So, it's you and me and the boys who are going to guide us. I just hope we don't run into a throng of cult members."

"We're good but being outnumbered will even up those odds pretty quickly." Lew had gone into contemplative detective mode. Vince stood silent, waiting for him to come up with his plan.

Lew bit his bottom lip. "The second we reach the field of mushrooms we send the boys packing. The way Lauren was talking about them, they'll be able to find their way back a lot easier than us."

He paused, staring into the forest. "If there is no activity we get out of the woods and try to find out where they are staging their ceremony."

He raised a finger as a counter point to his own line of thought. "Based on what you've said though, they believe the Wendigo to be at that location. So, it would make sense to start there and move outward. If we can get to the spot before they do, we'd have the element of surprise."

Vince opened his mouth to interject, but Lew continued, "But that's the problem of not knowing if they'll show up or not. We just have to hope they are there when we arrive. This is all the worst. Every bit of this. I feel like we made it to the championship game, but no one will tell us where we're supposed to play it, or what sport it is."

"And what do we do for the rest of the day? Sit around waiting for tomorrow? With no leads, no hints, no ideas? Is there anything else we can do?" Vince muttered.

Lew snapped his fingers. "Let me talk to him. We go back to your house, and I go talk to Martin alone."

Vince furrowed his brow. "Alone?"

Lew nodded. "Yeah. He thinks you're still on his side. If you question him, he'll doubt the validity of your claims. I don't think he ever genuinely believed I was one of the disciples. I could see it in his eyes."

"That could work. Maybe. For all the insanity hidden underneath, he still seems to be fairly bright. Whatever we do, we cannot release him until after tomorrow is all over." Vince stared intently at Lew for a long moment.

"Of course. He stays put until this is all over. I don't think he's going to talk, but it seems we are already grasping at straws, so we might as well try to build a raft to float on, no matter how rickety it is."

Vince laughed at how Lew always had some crazy analogy for the situation. If retirement were off the table for quite a few more years, he knew he would be partners with Lew until the badge and gun were slid across the table. Even if the dynamic had slightly shifted during this case.

"Why don't we head over there now? I'll fix us up a nice frozen dinner, and we can chat after you're all done. It'll give me a chance to try and relax for a few minutes."

Lew belted out a laugh, startling Vince once again. "You won't be relaxing. Neither of us will relax until the conclusion of our little tale."

Vince nodded, knowing that Lew spoke the truth. He climbed into his car, started it up, and headed back to his house, Lew following close behind. The sense of dread lingered, but Vince felt he had dispersed a small amount to his partner, sharing the burden.

4

Vince paced his living room, imagining all the things that could be happening in his shed out back. Lew could be torturing Martin or yelling at him or begging him to tell him anything. There was no way to know with Lew. The strength of knowledge between the partners had a lot to do with visual cues. Lew's mouth could be saying one thing, but one sly change on his face and Vince knew exactly what the intent was.

Here there was nothing visual or audible to clue Vince, only speculation. And everything he speculated was frightening. Nothing came out the way they wished. He had to sit and hope and try not to bounce his legs up and down until they fell off.

He opened and closed his freezer five times, trying to time out when to put the dinners in the microwave so it would coincide with Lew's entrance to the house. But there were no signals, nothing to alert Vince to his arrival. The door to the shed didn't even squeak.

After what felt like an hour, but had most likely only been fifteen minutes, Lew walked through the front door and walked right up to Vincent. He was shaking his head. He obviously had not gotten the information he was hoping for, but Vince wasn't about to let him stay silent on the visit.

"What did he say?" Vince asked anxiously.

"Religious rhetoric. Over and over. No matter what I said to him." Lew was breathing heavily, frustrated with the lack of progress he had made.

"What kind of rhetoric?"

"Oh, you know, the master will come tomorrow. He will return to full strength. Those who follow him will become like gods and those who deny him will fall." Lew threw his hands in the air.

"Nothing about where to find the field of mushrooms?" Vince was beginning to feel desperate again.

"He laughed and said that if I couldn't find the field it meant the master didn't trust me enough to know where it was. He basically called me a traitor to the cause, which, if this whole thing weren't so creepy, I would have been offended." Lew started to pace the living room.

"So, we've been stonewalled once again. Left with nothing but our gut."

"Yeah, and one of those guts has a special relationship with human flesh." Lew almost stopped his mouth from uttering the words, but they hung in the air like a balloon filled with poison gas.

"Oh, man, I'm sorry. I didn't mean—" Lew began to backpedal, but Vince smiled and looked at his partner.

"It's okay. I understand. It's very confusing. I hope that this *desire* goes away soon. I'll waste away before I feast on human flesh again. Continue."

Lew hesitated before continuing to pace. "He *did* inadvertently give me information that makes me believe they'll be out at this field tomorrow evening. *As the moon rises, the Wendigo shall return to full power and roam the earth, consuming the greed and filth of humanity.* At least we have that little tidbit."

Vince nodded, deep in thought. Lew noticed and stopped pacing. "What are you thinking?"

"If I am one of the chosen, wouldn't I be *called* to the Wendigo when the time is here?"

"But there *is* no Wendigo, so we can't rely on that." Vince could sense the tension and frustration building in Lew like a twisted-up rubber band and he needed to bring him down before it snapped.

"Okay, so we move forward according to our plan. We make sure we're both armed and aware of our surroundings at all times. Do you have ear buds for your phone? We can keep them on at all times and stay in constant communication." Vince brought Lew back with the procedural piece and he could see him calming.

"Yeah, I've got some buds I can put in for tomorrow. If we get separated, we call out our movements and positions. Basic police maneuvers. Check every corner and call out the *all clear*. The only sensible way to go about it."

Lew was back in his professional brain and that put Vince at ease; at least as much as was possible given the circumstances.

"I would say you could crash here, but we both need as much rest as possible. We need to be sharp."

Lew couldn't help but grin. "Okay, dad."

Vince waved the reply away. "I know, it's cheesy, but I need to make sure we're on our game. I don't care whether we face a gang of cultists or a mythological beast, I will be as prepared as possible."

Lew started to laugh. "Okay, okay. I get it. I'm going now. To go sleep. For tomorrow's battle."

He shook his head, laughed again and then unexpectedly reached out and hugged Vince. Words weren't needed. Vince returned the hug.

Lew left and Vince returned to his living room, pacing the floor. His stomach was in knots, and he was slightly fatigued. He truly noticed his weight loss for the first time. And he realized he was very hungry and had remained so ever since taking bites out of Martin's wrist.

He forced himself to go to his bedroom and lie down. His eyes refused to close until close to midnight, but when they did, he slept hard.

SEPTEMBER 22

1

Vince knew he was dreaming this time. He was running around the woods behind his house, searching for the onlookers, the disciples. And he thought he would catch a glimpse out of the corner of his eye, but when he turned there would be nothing except more trees.

He was aware of his rapid breathing, something pushing him onward in his search, a feeling that if he didn't find what he was looking for all would be lost. Another flash of movement; again, nothing.

Darting behind another tree he felt a hunger pang stab him in the gut. He needed food, but nothing satisfied. And he wasn't about to snack on any more people. Another sound behind him and he turned just in time to see a foot disappear behind the trunk of a tree. But the foot looked dead and necrotic. For some reason, the sight of it caused the hunger pangs to invade the dream again. Something about the foot was enticing. But it was also revolting. It looked almost diseased.

Finally giving up the search, he made his way toward the shed where Martin was being held. There was a padlock on the door, although he distinctly remembered there not being one in real life. That cemented that it was indeed a dream, which sent off alarm bells in his head, because he had no idea what he was about to encounter. He felt as though he were lucid enough to know he was dreaming, but not enough to control anything in the dream.

Using every ounce of energy he could muster, he tried to veer away from the shed, but his dream body continued along its path.

Reaching the door, he grabbed the lock in one hand and crushed it, disintegrating the metal between his fingers. He wrenched open the door and looked inside. Horror filled his mind as he realized that the entire shack was filled with body parts: arms, legs, heads, torsos, everything. They covered the entire floor and were piled in drifts in the corners. The revulsion almost made him throw up, but he wasn't sure if he would only throw up in the dream or in real life.

Something shifted and Vince looked around. His shed had transformed into something else; something resembling a rib cage. It had become alive, slight movements causing him to slowly rock back and forth as the rib cage rose and fell, like something was breathing.

In his attempt to figure out where he now was, he noticed something pulsating a short distance from him. It looked like a heart. Out of the corner of his eye he thought he glimpsed a face, the face of the Wendigo. He was staring intently at Vince, watching his every move.

A sudden urgency rushed over Vince, and he knew he needed to get to the heart and squeeze it until it stopped beating, or the Wendigo would devour him, and he would become one of the bodies laid out before him.

He began to walk over the body parts quickly, listening to the wet crunches as he snapped bones and squished muscle and tendon. When he got to the table, he stood on top of a small hill of human remains and began to methodically stomp them under his feet.

With each motion, he could feel the bodies break. His mouth watered as he thought of putting these pieces in his mouth and chewing. But he set aside those thoughts and focused on moving toward the heart, frustrated with how far away it remained.

As he stomped, trying to get traction enough to continue his journey, he began to hear the sound of someone screaming. It sounded as if they were a long way off, but it was a distinctly human sound. He began to jump up and down on the pile, angry with his inability to make progress, and the screaming intensified until finally he landed on a knee, snapping it backward. His feet sank quickly into the pile, and he struggled to keep his head above the rest of the bodies. He gasped for air, a wave of limbs cascading down upon him. He clamped his mouth shut as he was covered and woke up to the sound of a muffled scream that turned quickly into a gurgling sound.

2

Vince's eyes shot open as he sank his teeth into Martin's neck, cutting short the scream he had been trying to vocalize through the gag in his mouth. He severed the carotid with the bite and blood sprayed everywhere. Vince watched as the life left Martin's eyes. It was very quick, and as Vince came to the realization of what he had done, he backed away and saw that Martin's arms and legs had been broken, some of the bones shattered and poking through the skin.

He sat down heavily on the ground near the door and put a hand over his mouth. There was no way this was real. It had to still be a dream. He slapped himself hard across the face and when that didn't wake him up, he started to silently sob. Tears ran down his face, mixing with the blood, making it look like he had brutally murdered someone. Technically, he had.

Martin's body slumped to one side and thick, oozing blood slowly dripped to the floor. Vince had heard somewhere that for blood to continue to flow out of the body there had to be a pulse. Blood could not be pumped out of veins or arteries without a heartbeat. Mesmerized, he sat and watched the blood slowly drip to the floor until there were no more droplets. The blood began to congeal around the neck wound and Vince found himself finally able to move. He knew he needed to clean up the mess, and since it was still dark outside, he figured now was as good a time as any.

He gathered up a bunch of industrial garbage bags and laid them on the table. Then he grabbed the axe hanging on the back wall and set about the task of dismantling the body piece by piece. As he chopped, he felt himself growing hungry again, craving more of the human flesh. It was bizarre to him how he could be so intrigued yet just as repulsed by something simultaneously. He knew that eating another human was innately wrong, but he couldn't bring himself to stop thinking about it. Surely, it must be the effect of the mushrooms, but how could that last this long. It had been nearly two days since he last came in contact with them.

He finished with the body and dragged the bags into the woods behind his house where he started to dig various holes, burying parts of the body in different areas. He made sure the holes were deep enough to not attract the local wildlife. And when he was done the sun was peeking over the horizon.

After all the talk with Lew about being well-rested, he was exhausted and wasn't sure if he would be able to do what was needed. His brain was fuzzy, and paranoia was creeping in. He wasn't so much concerned about being caught, he simply did not want to get caught before he could stop the cult from achieving their goal, whatever it was.

After ensuring that everything was cleaned up, Vince walked back to his house and took a long shower. He turned the water to the hottest it would go and when he stepped out his skin was glowing from the heat.

Forgetting that everything tasted like clay to him, he made a breakfast of eggs, toast, bacon, and pancakes. He threw it all out after his first bite.

Making his way to the bedroom, he pulled out his service pistol and attached it to his hip. He made sure his badge was with him and shoved some pepper spray into his pocket.

Looking at the clock he realized it was nearly time to go pick up Lauren's nephews and try to end this thing. He grabbed his car keys and walked out of the house.

He remembered little of the morning's events after biting Martin's jugular.

3

Vince and Lew rode in silence all the way to the Tensley's house. It didn't appear that Lew had slept very well either. They were going to have to trust each other fully when they arrived out in the forest.

The Tensley's house was at the end of a long gravel driveway. Vince listened intently to the pop and crackle of the rocks squirting out from under the car's tires. He was trying hard to concentrate, but events kept slipping through his mind, and he was too tired to connect the dots.

They pulled up in front of the house and the two boys were sitting on the front porch enjoying a soda.

Vince and Lew exited the vehicle and Vince held up his badge so the boys could see. "Hello, I'm Detective Aronson, this is my partner Detective Monroe. Are you Andy and Matt?"

The older one nodded. Vince could see that neither of them appeared to be over the age of ten, which made him hope even more that they wouldn't have to witness any of the confrontation he was sure would be waiting for them in the woods.

Their father walked out the front door, still holding a backpack from their recent camping trip. "Lauren called. She told me what you need the boys to do for you."

"Yes sir. I want to make it abundantly clear they are not in trouble for taking the stones. We simply need help finding the spot they took them from." He turned to look at the boys. "You think you're up to the challenge?"

The younger of the two, Matt, stood up and blurted out, "Heck yeah. I know exactly how to get back there."

Mr. Tensley grabbed him by the shoulder and pulled him back

beside him. Vince could see that the dad was registering some level of danger in the request, but he stared Vince down to let him know he didn't want the boys to know.

"How about you boys go get our guests here something to drink before you head out."

Both boys eagerly ran into the house, and Mr. Tensley took three giant steps and got in Vince's face. "What kind of trouble you all facing out there?"

Vince allowed the discomfort of the proximity to grow. It helped Mr. Tensley feel like he had the upper hand. He had the dominance in the conversation.

"We have a group of cultists who are trying to make something happen this evening. We think it has to do with the clearing where your boys found the stones."

After a few tense seconds, Mr. Tensley took a step back, allowing a bit of distance between the two men. At that moment Andy and Matt came barreling out of the house holding sodas for each Detective.

"I would go with you, but I have a prior commitment. I am relying on you fellas to keep my boys safe. They'll get you where you need to go. I have no doubt," Mr. Tensley said loud enough for the boys to hear.

He took another step back and turned to Andy and Matt, putting a hand on each of their shoulders. Kneeling down in front of them he said, "I want you to listen to everything the Detectives say. If they tell you to run you run, if they tell you to stop you stop. Do you understand me?"

They both nodded and smiles crept onto their faces. Vince could sense the excitement in every movement. They were going to have stories to tell at school when this was all over.

Mr. Tensley reached out a hand and shook Vince's hand, adding a little extra pressure to ensure that Vince was aware that if anything happened to the boys, he didn't care that Vince was an officer of the law. He moved on to Lew and gave him the same handshake. Vince noticed that Lew winced slightly.

Vince saw that the boys were already moving to the car, and he nodded at Lew. Then Vince had a thought. "You boys still have those rocks you grabbed from the forest?"

Matt turned to Vince with a big smile on his face. "Of course. We've been so busy backpacking with dad that we didn't have a chance to take them out of the bag we put 'em in originally. We were going to sort through 'em this weekend and place 'em around the yard as decorations."

His face fell a little. "You want me to grab 'em?"

Vince nodded his head and replied, "Yeah. Probably best we put them back where they came from. Sorry about that."

Matt looked sad for a moment and then his brilliant smile returned to his face. "Nah, it's okay. Plenty of other rocks out there for us." And he ran into the house to grab the bag of stones.

He returned about a minute later, walking slower, the weight of the rocks apparent in how he held the bag. They put the sack in the trunk and the boys got in the backseat, making sure they buckled up immediately. Out of the corner of his eye, Vince saw them give each other high fives, and he smiled.

As they made their way back down the driveway, the crackling of the gravel sent flashes of images into Vince's head. Bones popping, a knee shattering backwards, Martin's neck erupting in a geyser of blood. He ran a hand over his face and noticed that Lew was looking at him, worried. Mustering his best smile, Vince shook his head to tell him there was nothing to be concerned about, and they turned onto the main road heading toward the forest.

4

By the time they made it to the forest entrance where the boys had started, Vince and Lew were convinced that children had an endless supply of questions from which to draw. It was only a ten-minute drive, but the boys had asked so many questions that Lew had resorted to repeating *I don't know* about everything that came out of their mouths.

"Here, here, here!" Andy yelled from the backseat, pointing at a small gap in the bushes about one-hundred feet in front of them. Vince pulled the car as close as he could to the trees, and they all hopped out.

"Hey!" Matt yelled. "Open up the trunk and I'll grab the stones."

Vince reached in the driver's side door and pulled a small lever, releasing the trunk latch. Andy grabbed the bag before his brother Matt could and slung the little knapsack over his shoulders, sticking his tongue out at his older brother.

The boys ran into the woods ahead of the Detectives, and only came back when Lew called out for them to *wait up for the old farts!* The boys had a good little giggle about that and then set off again, but this time checking behind them every ten seconds to make sure the *old farts* were still there.

Once in the forest, the boys quieted down considerably. They seemed to be concentrating on the paths they needed to take. To that end Vince watched as they navigated splitting paths without so much as a hesitation. There was no doubt they knew where they were going. An image flashed through his head, something about a lost girl in the woods. It was gone as quickly as it appeared.

They walked in near silence for more than two hours before Vince started to become nervous. There was no way this place was this deep in the forest. Another image flashed, a sort of time lapse showing the day slip into night the last time he was out here. And off went the visual into his subconscious once again.

"You boys think we could take a little rest? We have to be getting pretty close, right?" Vince puffed through the questions, his breath coming in short, sharp bursts.

Andy smiled, as if to convey how naïve Detective Aronson truly was. "We still have a ways to go. It's pretty deep in the woods. I remember it took us the better part of a day to get there and back."

Vince looked over at Lew and Lew spoke up, "Hey, guys, you wanna give us a second? I need to have a little chat with my partner."

Both boys nodded and moved off toward the far side of the little clearing where they had stopped. Andy handed the bag of stones over to his brother to carry for a while.

Lew stepped up to Vince and leaned in close. "I'm beginning to think sending them off on their way home by themselves isn't such a good idea," Vince whispered.

"I know what you mean, but what are we going to do about it now? We can't find our way to the clearing, and we can't turn back." Lew shook his head.

"We improvise. We tell the boys to let us know when the clearing is close and then make an excuse for them to place the stones back in the spots where they originally took them. When we are done, we head back and never come to these woods ever again." Vince tried to say the last part with a touch of levity, but it came across ominous.

"Sounds like a plan to me," Lew said to Vince. Then, raising his voice, he said, "Hey, boys. You ready to keep going? Let us know when we are really close to the clearing, won't you?"

The boys responded enthusiastically and resumed tracking their way toward their destination.

Another hour passed and the boys started to become slightly agitated. Vince could feel a shift in the atmosphere as well. Dread welled up in his chest and he could see that Lew felt something as well. The sun had started its afternoon descent and Vince felt that they were running out of time.

"How much longer, boys?" Vince asked with more intensity than he intended.

"I would say we're nearly there," Matt said, and looked to his brother for confirmation. When he got a slight head nod he added, "Definitely getting close."

"That's good. We appreciate you helping us out."

Andy turned his head slightly, and there was something slightly off about the look he gave Vince. "It's no problem. We enjoy exploring. It's fun."

Vince and Lew exchanged a look. Something was happening this far into the woods. Maybe it was exhaustion, but Vince imagined something more powerful was at play here. The air felt electrified, and the wildlife sounded like a record player skipping back a few seconds, repeating the same pieces over and over.

There was a rustling in the bushes, but the boys didn't seem to hear it. They continued to move forward, and it seemed that they were moving faster and faster, almost as if they were trying to lose Vince and Lew.

More rustling and a sweat broke out on Vince's forehead. He could swear there were now voices intermingled with all the other sounds; soft whispers incanting doom upon the travelers.

Vince looked over at Lew, but he didn't give any indication that he heard anything that was happening. The next thought that entered Vince's head was that he was hallucinating. This place had a power imbued through connection to the mushrooms. And he was the only one affected, because he was the only one encountered them.

Glancing from side to side, Vince began to see small movements in the undergrowth. Tails slithered under bushes, paws slipped behind tree trunks, silhouettes standing still and then moving out of focus. His breathing increased and he felt the forest closing in around him. The light from the sun was diminished and he squinted to see further into the darkness under the canopy.

The boys turned to glance at him periodically, and there was something sinister in their faces. He was afraid they were part of this whole thing. Everyone was. Even Lew. They were all in on it and he was the last holdout. If they couldn't convert him, they would kill him. His hand flashed to his gun holster, and he felt a hand close over his.

Lew pulled Vince close and whispered fiercely in his ear, "I've been watching you. Something is happening. I'm going to take your gun, so you don't accidentally kill one of those boys or me."

Vince looked at Lew with a vicious expression. "You want to kill me. I won't let you. You can't hurt me." He tried to pull away from Lew, but Lew held firm.

"I can feel the power of this place. It's intoxicating. But it is lying to you. Nothing it is telling you is the truth. We will find this cult and we will put a stop to it. I just need you to hold it together a little longer. That's all. Can you do that for me…partner?" Lew locked eyes with Vince and didn't look away.

Vince stared back and finally nodded his head, relaxing his gun hand. "You take it. If I touch it none of this ends well."

Lew secretly slipped the holster off Vince's belt and tucked it into his own belt opposite his personal gun. The boys looked back, smiled and said in unison, "Just a few more minutes and we'll be there."

Vince's fists clenched and Lew put a hand on his shoulder, trying to ground him to reality. The boys snickered and whispered to each other.

Vince was sure they were still conspiring against him. And he could see shapes pacing them as they got closer to the clearing. They had a shadowy escort, and it didn't do a thing to help Vince's nerves. He felt that if he opened his eyes any wider, they would melt out of his skull, and everyone would abandon him in the forest to fend for himself. Everything was so hot, which made no sense to Vince. It should be getting cooler, not hotter. And that wriggling had intensified in his head. He had no idea what was happening, and he started to panic.

Turning to Lew he was about to express his concerns when he ran into the back of one of the boys. He nearly fell but caught himself and looked at the boys suspiciously. "Why did you stop?" Vince asked with a sharp tone in his voice.

Andy and Matt looked at each other and then at Lew, who shot them a sympathetic look in return. "You see that archway over there?" Matt pointed at a bush that seemed to have grown up and over a path.

Vince nodded his head, feeling a surge of energy emanating from that space. "That's it? Right through there?"

The boys nodded and took a step back. "We don't want to go in there. There's something bad in there."

Vince nodded his head. "I understand. And that's all right. Thank you for getting us this far. We can take it from here."

Lew smiled and grabbed Vince gently by the arm. They turned away from the boys so they could have a private conversation. "You still want them to do that little job?"

At first Vince was confused. He thought their job was getting them here. Then Lew raised his eyebrows, tilted his head and mouthed the word, *stones.*

Turning, Vince said, "If you boys would like a—" And that was as far as he made it. The area where they had all been standing was empty. Only Vince, Lew, and the bag filled with rocks remained.

Lew pushed past Vince and scanned the immediate area. He put his hands to his mouth and yelled, "Andy! Matt! Where did you go? Come on back!"

Vince and Lew both held their breaths, waiting for a response, but when there was none, they panicked and searched the footprints for any clues of where they may have run off to. But the ground was hard, and footprints held no claim.

Lew grabbed his hair in his hands and looked anxiously at Vince. "What do we do? What do we do now?"

Vince, in a moment of clarity, took a deep breath, stared intently at Lew, and said, "We finish what we came here to do. We find this cult and we end them. Plain and simple." He picked up the rocks, noting their weight and finding himself impressed the boys lugged them as far as they had.

Lew gestured at the forest. "But the boys…"

Vince shook his head. "There is nothing we can do for them right now. If we search for them, we get lost ourselves. And I don't want to get lost out here. Not again."

Lew's breathing slowed and he nodded his head slowly. "Yeah, that makes sense. We need to think about this rationally. We do what we need to do and when we get back, we send out a search party. That's what needs to happen."

Vince smiled. "That's what needs to happen."

Both men had regained their composure and they looked at the little arch that stood about fifty feet away. With renewed purpose they walked a little deeper into the woods to solve their case.

5

The two men ducked under the low arch and stepped into a clearing. Vince still clutched the bag of stones tightly. They had no idea what to expect, and at first there was nothing out of the ordinary. Vince had cleared his head enough to be able to focus on their task. Lew looked around anxiously, expecting an attack from anywhere.

Vince absentmindedly reached inside the bag and pulled out one of the rocks. It was beautiful. There were etchings on the face of the stone, and it had been sanded to absolute smoothness. He ran his fingers along the swirls and ancient hieroglyphs. There was no way to be certain if what was etched into the rock was an ancient language, or simply drawings. Somehow it didn't matter in Vince's head. They were wonderfully ornate, and he found himself wishing they didn't have to leave them out here.

Lew nudged his shoulder and Vince looked up at him. Vince allowed Lew to take the bag from him, but he kept hold of the one he had removed. He felt like he was underwater, and everything was moving in slow motion. Lew nudged him again and Vince shook his head clear.

They took a few more steps into the clearing and stopped dead in their tracks. Up ahead of them was a grouping of posts sticking out of the ground. On those posts hung five people. They had been flayed open and all their heads were lolling. Blood trickled from wounds and Vince and Lew slowly approached the gruesome scene.

As they neared the first person, they heard a gasp. One of the other people had inhaled deeply, and was now coughing, blood spurting out with each hack. Vince rushed up beside him and called out to him. "Hey! Who did this to you? Where did they go? We can help you."

The man looked at Vince and the look of pain was covered over by pure ecstasy. A smile grew on his face, revealing blood-stained teeth. "It's you!" he exclaimed. "Leader of the disciples. Welcome. We've been awaiting your arrival."

A couple more breaths could be heard nearby, and Vince and Lew looked around to find the sources. One woman and one man opened their eyes and stared longingly at Vince.

"You have arrived! Thank the Master," the woman said, deep veneration in her voice.

The other man got too excited and began coughing up blood. Vince moved toward him. "Let me help you. I'll get you down from there. We can get you medical attention." He pulled out his cell phone and saw he had no bars.

Vince reached up toward the man and the man tried to wiggle away from his grasp. "What are you doing, leader? Why do you condemn me?"

Lew had moved up and was trying to figure out how to safely get the man down from the post. "What are you talking about? If you stay up there you will die."

"It would be my honor to die for the Master," the man said. Vince and Lew heard the other two echo the sentiment. "I chose this ending so that others might thrive in the presence of the Master."

Vince's head began to throb. He reached out in one last attempt to help the man, but the man cried out, a look of understanding dawning on his face. "You are a false leader. You do not believe in the Master's plan. You are a trickster, a spy, an enemy."

The other two caught wind of the diatribe and piped in with their own accusations. Vince backed into the center of the posts and spun around, looking at the five men and women hanging, some dead, some dying. He covered his ears, yelling as loud as he could. They scoffed at him. And then the stone he had been holding slipped from his grasp, tumbling to the ground, and all three of them went silent instantly.

It took Vince a moment to realize what had happened, but when he did, he looked over at Lew, an idea brewing. He moved toward Lew and as he did, the three still alive on the posts watched him closely. It seemed as though they wanted to speak, but none of them dared.

Leaning in close to Lew, Vince whispered in his ear, "They are treating the stones like they have some sort of power. Maybe if we place them around the clearing, we can get them to stop long enough to catch the other members by surprise."

Lew nodded his head and thrust his hand inside the bag. Vince picked up the stone he had dropped and approached the woman, holding it out in front of her. She began to writhe, her mouth open in a silent scream. He moved to one of the men and got a similar result. He was suddenly very relieved he had asked the boys to bring them along.

Lew began placing stones in and around the patches of mushrooms, trying to hold his breath, but failing. He wasn't sure if any of the spores were getting to him, but there was a sense of urgency that belayed that fear. He had a job to do. In a few spots there were vague impressions in the ground where the rocks had most likely been before they were removed. Lew attempted to get the stones as close to their original positioning as possible.

Vince turned away from the posts but felt himself pulled back toward them. The energy was strongest in the middle of the human sacrifices. He stepped back into the center and looked around, realizing the posts hadn't been placed randomly, there was a pattern to them. He saw a small rise nearby and ran over to it. With even that little bit of height he recognized that the sacrifices were placed in the shape of a pentagram.

He heard the whisper a moment before he was about to head back toward Lew, who was still placing totems at various intervals around the clearing. "You disappoint me, Vincent."

Vince whirled around, looking for the source of the voice.

It spoke again, from another location in the clearing, "You have strength, and I thought it could be used to build for the future."

Vince spun again, but all he saw was Lew wandering around and the people on the posts hanging limply. It seemed they had all finally died. Lew hadn't heard the voice speaking to him.

"Stop talking to me," Vince said to the clearing.

"I told you that time was infinite, and infinite was all time. You could have ruled the universe alongside me. You could have had ultimate power." The whisper was soothing.

"It is not too late, you know. Stop your partner from placing those stones and join me. We will feast for all eternity."

"No!" Vince whispered fiercely.

He began to walk toward Lew and Lew held his hands up to indicate he had finished his part. Vince nodded to him, hoping to place the last stone and be done with whatever evil lurked in this part of the forest.

As he reached the posts, he heard the voice one last time as a rumbling in his chest. "So be it!"

The rumbles continued along the ground and into the far area of the clearing, where a massive shape stood from sitting, rising until its head rose among the treetops. The Wendigo was here after all. Surrounding him were the girls, the ones he had held hands with and who served as mouthpiece for the ancient being.

Vince watched as the beast slowly absorbed the energy from his conduits, the girls withering away until they dissipated in a whirlwind of ash. With each girl he moved closer to where Lew and Vince stood. Lew was saying something to Vince, but it was muffled to him. He was fully mesmerized by the being he had nearly convinced himself didn't exist.

Finally, Lew noticed that Vince wasn't looking at him and he turned around and craned his neck up toward the top of the canopy of trees. He stopped moving and inhaled sharply, his knees almost giving out on him.

"What is that?!" he screamed.

Vince watched as Lew found his legs and started to back pedal toward Vince. They met each other in the center of the sacrifices, both looking terrified. "I guess I really did meet the Wendigo, eh partner?"

Lew looked at Vince with terror on his face. He sneezed twice in quick succession and rubbed his nose. Vince could tell that his brain was having trouble comprehending the being in front of them.

They watched as the Wendigo absorbed the next girls and moved even closer. There were only a few remaining and Vince had the suspicion it would have enough energy to move to the sacrificial circle. Maybe if he knocked them down it would slow his progress. He moved to the first post and set the Totem on the ground. Leaning with all his weight, Vince strained to move the post, but it wouldn't budge. He slammed his body against it but only succeeded in jiggling the body enough to make wet, smacking noises as the flesh connected with the wood.

Lew stepped up beside him and said, "No! Stop. Toss me the stone. I will end this."

Vince took a step away from Lew and clutched the stone to his chest, eyeing Lew suspiciously. "I've got this. Don't you trust me,

Lew? I'm your partner. You trust me, right?"

Lew looked away and didn't answer. Vince brushed past him and walked toward the Wendigo, who was now kneeling to come face-to-face with Vince. The Wendigo's eyes rolled around in their sockets and the creaks and groans from the skeletal form of the creature sent chills down Vince's spine.

A vicious smile formed on the Wendigo's face as his eyes stared through Vince. For a moment Vince was mesmerized. Then Lew grabbed him from behind and spun him around, always keeping one eye on the creature. Fear emanated from Lew. The power of this place had frightened him beyond belief.

"Where do we need to place the rock? I can do it. I placed the rest. Let me finish this."

Vince shoved him. "I will finish this. I'm the one that had to deal with the Wendigo before. I'm the one that will seal the Wendigo back inside his prison."

He clapped Lew on the shoulder and smiled at him warmly. "Without the Wendigo to lead them, the followers will be lost. They'll no longer have anything to fight for. We solved the case. It's over as soon as I place this last stone."

Vince was confused as to why Lew was struggling with him. Didn't they want the same outcome? Maybe Lew had truly become a disciple of the Wendigo and had been playing him this whole time. Any rational person wouldn't have gone along with a plan to kidnap someone and then calmly stand by while their partner and friend bit into that person. He was played and he didn't even see it. How stupid could he be!

Lew watched Vince warily as Vince swayed back and forth on his feet. It felt like something was crawling around inside of him, trying to find an exit. It was the Wendigo, attempting to gain control over

Vince again. He wasn't about to let that happen.

Vince turned and stared directly at the Wendigo as another girl disintegrated. He could feel its power grow.

"You do not control me. I will end you. Right here, right now!"

The Wendigo let out a grating wail that sounded like teeth grinding together. Vince turned back to Lew, who was holding out his gun in front of him.

Vince laughed and said, "I highly doubt that will do anything against it, but you are more than welcome to try."

Lew licked his lips, his grip tightening and retightening on the gun. His breathing was steady, but quick. There was a flicker of madness in his eyes. For a moment Vince wasn't sure if his partner was aiming the gun at the Wendigo or at him.

"I need you to move, Vincent. Right now."

Vince looked over his shoulder and realized that the Wendigo was hunched right behind him. Lew had no shot at the creature with Vince standing in the way.

Vince laughed again and said, "Oh, of course. Let me move out of the way."

This all seemed so suddenly absurd. A twinge of anger wound its way through Vince's body.

Everything happened in a flash. As Vince moved out of the way he noticed that the Wendigo finished absorbing the energy of the last girl and Lew leapt forward, pushing Vince out of the way, yelling, "No! Don't do it!" at the Wendigo.

Vince went sprawling, but somehow managed to hold onto the stone. The Wendigo swung his arm, connecting with Lew's temple, crushing his skull with a wet, crunching sound. Vince yelled out and rushed to Lew's side, checking him for vitals, still holding fast to the stone. Blood gushed down the side of Lew's face and Vince futilely tried to staunch the flow, unaware the rock was still in his grasp and running slick with blood. Any suspicions of Lew having turned against him were destroyed in an instant.

"Lew! Lew! Don't leave me, buddy! Stay with me! I need you to stay with me!" Vince yelled into his crushed face.

Lew lurched one time, blood spraying out of his mouth, one eye rolling loosely in its socket. And then he was gone, one final gurgling breath escaping his mouth.

Vince looked up, tears streaming down his face, and saw the Wendigo standing above him. The Wendigo rose to full height and raised its foot to bring down and smash Vince. Without thinking, Vince set the stone on the ground next to Lew and raised his hands to protect himself. He closed his eyes, waiting for the beast to stomp the life out of him.

When nothing happened, Vince opened his eyes, astonished at what he saw. Roots shot out of the ground, wrapping around the Wendigo's arms and legs, pulling him backward and onto the ground. Vince watched with horrified fascination as the Wendigo was pulled by the roots to the earth and then into the giant patch of mushrooms. The Wendigo struggled, releasing a loud roar into the air that shook Vince to his core. For a moment it seemed as though the Wendigo was successfully pulling against the roots, but with one final tug, he fell to the ground. His hands clawed at the ground, leaving deep gouges in the dirt. He let out a massive roar once again and the last Vince saw of the Wendigo were its eyes staring hatefully at him. And then he was gone, leaving only the mushrooms behind. It didn't appear that they had been disturbed at all.

It was over. The foul creature had been defeated. Vince looked around the clearing, breathing heavily. All around him was death. Five people hanging from posts. Lew dead in front of him. No sign left of the Wendigo.

Vince stood up, lurched to one side and vomited onto the ground. Something long and gooey came out of his body with the puddle of bile. He was certain he saw it wriggle once and then it lay still. He felt better. His head was clearing. There was nothing left to do but leave the forest.

In his shock, Vince reached down and grabbed Lew's hand and began to drag him out of the clearing and through the arch. He dragged Lew for hours, the forest pitch black by the time he found his way out. His car sat ten feet in front of him and he sat down on the ground, releasing Lew's hand. He didn't notice that his friend was almost unrecognizable because of the arduous journey through the woods.

Vince took out his cell phone and dialed a number. He listened to the phone ring and when someone picked up on the other side, he said, "Yeah, I need someone to come out and help me. My partner has been killed. And there's a bunch of people deep in the forest who were used as sacrifices."

He listened for a few seconds and then nodded his head. "Yeah, I'll keep my phone on. Just follow the GPS."

He pressed end on the phone and scooted over to his car, leaning against the bumper, feeling the exhaustion of the week. He had won *and* he had lost, and it was over. The Wendigo would never terrorize anyone again. And that was good enough for him. It had to be.

AUTHOR'S NOTE

When I set out to write this book, I knew there would be a sticky point when it came to introducing characters that are First Nations. I wanted to ensure I was being respectful of their culture and not falling into the trappings of stereotypes, and I hope I have accomplished that within the story.

A huge thank you to my Beta readers who always give me invaluable feedback when it comes to fleshing out the story in a way that entertains and intrigues people. My brother Chad, the two Samanthas, the double Pauls, and Margaret. Thank you to Felix for helping me discover better ways to incorporate the First Nations characters, and for the beautiful blurb on the cover of the book.

And, as always, thank you to the people who support me wholeheartedly including my extended family and my wife, Renee, who is my biggest encouragement and continues to make sure I know where my talent and abilities are.

THE WOOD WILL SWALLOW YOU WHOLE

COMING SOON

TURN THE PAGE FOR A SHORT STORY FROM
THIS COLLECTION

ALL THE LAND YOU OWN

You own a plot of land. On this plot of land there is a pond. In this pond lives a school of fish, a whole host of frogs, and an underwater treasure. A Great heron visits the pond once a day to scoop up one of the fish, yet the number never dwindles.

One day, as you walk your land you notice a tear in the ground. It isn't that some machine has come through and tilled up the soil. It's more of a gaping wound that has not been sewn back together with sutures. This tear makes you sad. It reminds you that life is fragile and even the earth beneath your feet is not immune to the violence of existence.

You follow the tear and discover that it leads directly to the pond. The gouge is below the water line, yet none of the water splashes over onto this ground. It's as if someone has placed a sheet of glass between the water and the dirt to hold it in place.

Curiosity takes hold and you return to your house to find a pickaxe and shovel. But as you walk you find yourself getting turned around. The common path you are used to walking every day becomes muddled in your head. It's like someone is rearranging thoughts in your brain to purposefully confuse you.

You stop.

You take a deep breath.

You allow your thoughts to coalesce into remembrance and then you continue your journey.

As you wander you see all the land you have tilled and dug into. The pieces of land you avoid because they remind you of something horrible and destructive. A shiver convulses your body, and your mouth runs dry.

How long have you been walking?

You don't ever recall it taking this long to walk from the pond to your house before.

In the distance you see the structure you are striving for, and a sense of relief falls over you. It isn't until this moment you realize your heart is beating too fast in your chest.

Although the house is within your eyesight you sit to take a rest.

You listen to the sounds of nature.

It is soothing.

You recall fishing in a lake when you were a child; your father next to you; a million gnats buzzing around your head.

But now you have aged, and you can feel the cold settle into your bones and aches come and go without so much as an invitation.

You can't recall what you were going to the house for, but hunger hits you like a brick wall. If you don't eat something soon you know you will feel faint and perhaps even pass out as your blood sugar plummets. So, you pick yourself up off the ground and continue your journey to the house.

A patch of unfamiliar ground rises in front of you, and you furrow your brow trying to remember the last time you came this way on your land.

You question if you've ever approached the house from this particular angle before, but you cannot recall.

At least you can see the house from here, so you can reach your destination.

Finally, after what feels like ages, your hand touches the familiar chill of the knob attached to the front door. You step inside, but immediately sense something is wrong. Although you cannot recall how long you have lived on this land by yourself, you know it has been quite some time.

There are picture frames lining the walls of the entryway, smiling faces you seem to know watching you walk toward the kitchen. They are vaguely familiar, but the names elude you.

Now that you are in the house you have lost track of the task you originally intended to accomplish. Instead of worrying about it, you decide to make yourself a sandwich, but when you search for a butter knife you discover that everything has been rearranged in the drawers, which makes no sense, since you live here alone, and no one ever comes to visit.

The anger takes hold and you fling drawers open, throwing them to the ground, watching utensils and pens and rubber bands and papers crash to the floor in a tumult of sound that makes you cover your ears in self-preservation.

You throw open the fridge and stand in front of the artificial light, wolfing down lunch meat and cheese until the dryness in your throat demands resolution as the choking feeling almost overwhelms you. And you rummage through the cabinets but are unable to find a single glass to fill.

The rage builds inside once again as you wonder exactly who in hell could have moved your items around.

As the fury subsides, you walk to the sink, dip your head under the running faucet, and drink deeply until your throat is no longer scratchy.

This act reminds you of your original intent with coming up to the house and you grab a pickaxe and a shovel and head back outside.

Upon your return to the pond, you notice that the tear has deepened, and yet still none of the water has leaked into the culvert. You imagine that if you could somehow allow the water to pass through to the dry earth all will be all right.

You put your hand against the invisible barrier between water and dirt and feel the pressure there.

It is almost unbearable.

So, you begin to work the ground, creating more space for the water to rush to, but no matter how much room you create, the water holds its shape and refuses to spill over and dampen the earth.

As you investigate this strange anomaly you notice a small wooden box nestled in a tangle of underwater weeds and rocks.

It looks old and warped.

Worn away from years of neglect.

You remove your shoes and socks and roll up your pant legs and wade into the pond. Fish scurry away, leaving bubble trails in their wake. Frogs hope from rock to rock, croaking in disapproval at the disturbance.

The water gets deeper and deeper until you realize your chest is under the surface. You feel around with your toes until they graze the top of the box.

Without hesitation you dive, looking for the exact spot your foot landed on moments before.

There is no air in your lungs. It feels as though you have forgotten the mechanics of breathing while simultaneously understanding that if you were to achieve the breath you so desperately need you would drown.

But the box persists.

As do you.

Panic begins to overcome you, but still, you struggle with the box.

Then your finger finds a latch and you open the box, needing to see what treasure lies within, even if it takes your last breath. And as the lid opens on its hinges you hear a melody. Something you haven't heard in years, possibly decades.

Pictures float out of the box, and you grab onto them as they pass by, floating to the surface.

And you know the faces in the photos.

They beckon for you to follow them to the surface, and you obey.

The sensation of flowing water tugs at your clothing, and you realize that the invisible dam has burst open, and the pond is expanding to heal the tear.

As you emerge from the water you realize you do in fact remember how to breathe and you inhale a lung full of air, grasping the photos tight in your fist.

And the melody persists, reminding you of everything you have ever forgotten.

Your house swims into focus and you recall where everything should be, and is, and you begin to cry.

Clarity rushes in and you hold tight to the memories.

An impending sense of déjà vu overwhelms you and as you trudge back to your home you pray that if you are cursed to repeat the same day over again, that you remember how to breathe.